GIVING

UP THE

GHOST

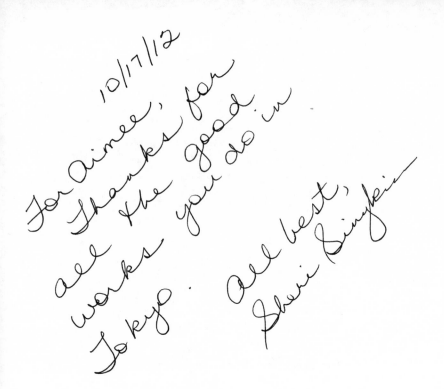

10/17/12

For Aimee,
Thanks for
all the good.
works you do in
Tokyo.   All best,
          Sheri Singkin

GIVING

UP THE

GHOST

SHERI SINYKIN

PEACHTREE
ATLANTA

Ω

Published by
PEACHTREE PUBLISHERS
1700 Chattahoochee Avenue
Atlanta, Georgia 30318-2112
www.peachtree-online.com

Text © 2007 by Sheri Sinykin
Cover photo © 2007 by Karekin Goekjian

First trade paperback edition published in 2011

Cover design by Loraine M. Joyner
Book design by Melanie McMahon Ives

Printed in the United States of America in January 2011 in Bloomsburg, PA,
by RR Donnelley & Sons
10 9 8 7 6 5 4 3 2 (hardcover)
10 9 8 7 6 5 4 3 2 1 (trade paperback)

Library of Congress Cataloging-in-Publication Data

Sinykin, Sheri Cooper.
  Giving up the ghost / by Sheri Sinykin. -- 1st ed.
      p. cm.
  Summary: Thirteen-year-old Davia encounters the ghost of a long-dead
young relative and comes to terms with her fears about her mother's can-
cer while helping to provide hospice care for her elderly, terminally ill
great-aunt at a Louisiana plantation.
  ISBN 978-1-56145-423-5 / 1-56145-423-0 (hardcover)
  ISBN 978-1-56145-572-0 / 1-56145-572-5 (trade paperback)
[1. Ghosts--Fiction. 2. Haunted places--Fiction. 3. Great-aunts--Fiction. 4.
Cancer--Fiction. 5. Death--Fiction. 6. Louisiana--Fiction.] I. Title.
  PZ7.S6194Gi 2007
  [Fic]--dc22
                                             2007019592

With love and gratitude to my brother, Loren,
and in memory of our mother,
Barbara "Bobbye" Kresteller Cooper,
whose passing we were blessed to share—
together with my husband Daniel
and our children, Aaron and Debbie Sinykin—
on February 20, 2006.

Special thanks to my Vermont College MFA advisors—
Louise Hawes, Ron Koertge, Carolyn Coman, and Marion
Dane Bauer; to my classmates for their honesty and feed-
back in workshops; to Sarah Lamstein, Toni DePalma
Palmerio, and Sally Riley for their continued friendship and
support long after our graduation; to Judy Hancock, cousin
by birth, sister by choice; to Norman and Sand Marmillion,
owners of Laura Plantation in Vacherie, Louisiana; to the
staff at the New Orleans Pharmacy Museum; to Dr.
Jonathan Hake, my mother's extraordinary cancer support
group leader in Folsom, CA; to play therapist Teri V. Krull,
LCSW, LLC, Mesa, AZ; to Julia C. Sinykin, for so carefully
reading drafts of my manuscript; to my insightful editor,
Lisa Mathews; and with gratitude and appreciation for
hospices everywhere, especially HospiceCare Inc.
(Madison, WI), where I was trained as a volunteer; Sutter
VNA & Hospice (Sacramento, CA); and Banner Hospice
(Gilbert, AZ), whose staff helped us care for my mother in
her last months of life.

CHAPTER 1

We're here," Dad said. *Finally.* The thousand-mile drive from Wisconsin to Louisiana had felt more like a million. Davia closed her summer journal and looked out the window with new interest.

From River Road, long beards of Spanish moss hung from two rows of gigantic oak trees that led up to a weathered plantation house. Brick columns, like stilts, seemed to lift the building off the ground. The whole place looked completely abandoned.

This can't be it, Davia thought. The big house wasn't at all what she'd been imagining—something more like Tara at the beginning of *Gone with the Wind.*

As the car pulled closer, she saw that the mansion needed paint. Badly. She couldn't even tell what color it had once been. And look at that sagging, wraparound porch. Had Katrina's floodwaters from the nearby Mississippi passed beneath the entire house two years ago? Maybe those weird stilts had saved it from being washed away.

"Aunt Mari lives in there?" Davia asked.

"She used to," Mom said, "till she got too sick and couldn't manage the stairs. Now she lives in the stable."

"The stable?" Davia's parents had described her great-aunt as a bit eccentric, but living among hay and horses sounded ridiculous even for Aunt Mari.

"Okay, it *used* to be a stable," Mom corrected herself. "It's been remodeled, so now it's more like an apartment, I guess. All on one level."

Dad followed the drive around back, while Davia scanned the grounds for the "beautiful forest" the place was named after in French. But she saw nothing even close to a dense growth of trees, besides the grand alley of oaks at the entrance. Just weeds. "So much for *Belle Forêt*," she said. "No *forêt* is more like it."

"There were probably plenty of trees years ago," Dad said. "Cypress, no doubt. Over in the swamp."

"The swamp?" She thought of the list in her journal of "Things I, Davia Ann Peters, Am Really Afraid Of." Snakes was Number Eight. Alligators was Number Twelve. So much for taking any walks around the grounds.

Dad turned toward her and grinned.

"Don't you dare laugh," Davia said. "You won't even be here to protect us."

"Sorry," Dad said. "Duty calls."

"Doesn't it always?" She flashed a semisweet smile in the direction of the rearview mirror. Then she glanced over at Mom, wondering what she thought about Dad spending most of each week with a Tulane professor friend, helping to restore houses. What if she and Mom needed help?

"I know you said you wanted to stay with Mom and Aunt Mari," Dad began, "but—"

"You could have gone to French camp," Mom cut in. "If you've changed your mind, honey, just let us know."

Davia looked down at the hangnail she'd recently begun picking. Of course she'd rather be at French camp, but that wasn't the point. She thought back to the last session with the therapist her parents had made her start seeing a couple of years ago. Hadn't Miss Teri said the worst thing for Davia would be separation from Mom right now?

"You really ought to stay with me in the city for a few days, Davia," Dad said. "We could check out Lafayette Cemetery and see where our most famous relative is buried."

Davia rolled her eyes. Sam Peters, father of the New Orleans public school system? Big whoop. There was no way she wanted to set foot in another cemetery. And there was no way she was ready yet to check out a city where so many people had suffered after Hurricane Katrina. For her own sake, she'd needed to try to put the TV images of the storm's aftermath on the back burner of her mind. Why couldn't Dad understand she wasn't here on some kind of vacation? She had to help Mom take care of Aunt Mari. End of story.

"Okay. Skip the cemetery. There's a great aquarium, and maybe we could take a swamp tour."

"Daddy," she protested.

"A river cruise?" he said.

There was nothing he could tempt her with in New Orleans. But what awaited her in the stable— a weird, dying old lady she'd never met—wasn't exactly tempting, either. She pictured Aunt Mari all shriveled up like a dried apple, moaning and crying, tubes going in and out of her. What would she say to someone like that? How could she even look at her? The whole idea creeped her out.

"We could get beignets in the French Quarter," Dad went on.

"Kenneth…" Mom began in a warning tone.

"I could make us an appointment to visit the pharmacy museum. You'd love it—it's got all these old medical instruments and—"

"Really? " Davia said, perking up, but she saw Mom shoot her father one of those *Please don't do this again* looks. Dad shrugged and said nothing.

Davia settled back in her seat, still thinking about that museum.

Mom nervously patted her hair, super-curly and graying now, as if she wanted to make sure it was still there—her own—and not a wig anymore. "What if Davia has an asthma attack?" she said finally. "Or heatstroke? Would you even know what to do?"

Dad looked straight ahead. "She'll be fine, Katie. Stop smothering the poor kid."

Go, Dad, Davia thought. She wasn't even convinced she had asthma anymore. That pharmacy museum sounded pretty cool—and maybe she and Dad could have special time together, for a change.

She begged Mom with her eyes, but Mom wouldn't look at her. She didn't have to. Her slumping shoulders said it all.

Davia felt like the Amazing Human Rubber Band, with Dad tugging on one side and Mom on the other. And though neither said a word, Davia knew Dad would let go, like always, and then she'd end up snapping back to Mom. After everything her mother had been through the last couple of years, how could she or Dad even think of leaving Mom here alone?

"Maybe another time, Davia," Dad said finally.

Mom reached over and touched his shoulder. Dad gave her a lopsided smile and slowed the car alongside a funny little two-story building with six sides. Its roof sloped gently upward, like the cap on an acorn. The lower level had high arches and a few open black shutters. Upstairs, the windows were shuttered as well.

"Not here." Mom waved Dad on. "I bet this is the *garçonnière*. It's absolutely charming, isn't it?"

Garçon, Davia knew, meant "boy" or "waiter" in French. What was this? A house for boy-waiters?

"Quite the bachelor pad, isn't it?" Dad sounded impressed.

"What?"

"The Creoles, Davia." Dad was using that teacher-tone that made her crazy sometimes, the same one he used to lecture his students—or to tell her and Mom about those PBS specials he watched alone at night in his study. "They were the descendants of the original French settlers in Louisiana. Remember? I'm sure I told you this before."

"Yeah, I guess so," Davia said.

"Anyway, a *garçonnière* is where they sent their rowdy teenage boys."

"To live?"

Dad nodded. "Yep. They kicked their own sons out of the house so they wouldn't bother anyone."

Davia's cat, GG, stirred in her crate, jingling her collar tags and bell. She'd been living on tranquilizers for the past two days just to survive the road trip. Davia poked her finger through the metal door grid and stroked GG's paw, the only thing she could reach. In a way, she liked GG too doped up to shy away from her. All she'd ever wanted when she picked her out at the cat show was a lovable blue-gray Tonkinese kitten—usually the most playful and "dog-like" of purebred cats. But not GG. She had grown up to be afraid of anything that moved.

"That must be the stable." Mom pointed to a long, red building to the right, opposite the *garçon-nière*. A small, beat-up car was parked alongside. It was plastered with bumper stickers like the one with the Grateful Dead bears and one that said "My husband is an honor student at obedience school." How weird *was* Aunt Mari, anyway? And what had happened to her husband?

Dad parked the minivan behind the car. "Everyone out!" he sang, as if they'd just arrived at Disney World.

As Davia slid open the door, a blast of heat plowed into the van, shoving her breath to the back of her throat. When she tried to breathe again, a hot, moist vapor threatened to suffocate her. Wisconsin had humidity in the summer, but nothing like this. Stupid air. Stupid South. Before Mom could blame the breathing difficulty on asthma, Davia fished her inhaler out of her backpack and took two quick puffs. No help at all. She heaved another labored breath, not yet ready to panic. "Welcome to Louisiana," the sign at the border should have read. "SCUBA gear required."

How did anyone breathe here? Davia felt like she was trying to suck air through a clogged straw. This kind of heat seemed un-survivable. Already, sweat was beading on her forehead. It inched toward her eyes. Her hair—thick and wavy and as dark as Mom's used to be—cried out for something to get it off her neck.

"Are you okay back there?" Three fine worry lines formed between Mom's pale, new eyebrows. Davia knew her mother was trying to sound casual.

"I can't breathe this air. Is Aunt Mari on oxygen? Maybe she'll share."

"Davia," Dad said. "Cut the drama. It's called high humidity."

Mom reached back and cradled Davia's chin in her hand. "You'll get used to it, hon. Just take it slow."

She didn't want to get used to it. All at once, she longed for a regular summer vacation. When she wasn't away at French camp, she and her parents had always done something special—concerts on the Square, canoeing on Lake Wingra, biking through the Arboretum. Once, before Mom got sick three years ago, they went from lighthouse to light-house, camping along the Great Lakes. Another time they'd overdosed on musicals in New York City—five in three days. And now this. Why hadn't she given more thought to what she'd do around here while Mom took care of Aunt Mari? She'd only brought so many books, and *Belle Forêt* seemed a long way from any library. A long way from anything but the Mississippi River.

Dad hopped out and opened the back hatch. "Hurry up, ladies," he said. "Let's get this stuff inside. Aunt Mari's bound to have air conditioning."

That was welcome news. Davia took the cat crate and dragged her suitcase to the front door, puffing like a weight lifter. Too bad all those pounds she'd put on during Mom's chemo treatments weren't muscle. Any time now, Mom kept saying, Davia was going to get her growth spurt and then she'd be fine. Davia was keeping her fingers crossed.

Mom rapped on the door with the brass knocker.

An older woman with short, permed-blonde hair greeted them. "You must be the Peters family," she said. "I'm Sara, Mari's hospice volunteer."

Aha, Davia thought. The car with the bumper stickers was probably hers.

"She's been asking for you. Mari's gonna be real glad to see y'all."

"Same here." Mom's eyes seemed shiny. "It's been far too long."

Davia hurried into the delicious cool air, and helped Dad move their bags into the bedroom Sara showed them. It had only one big bed in it. Davia looked around for a cot or an air mattress.

As if reading her mind, Sara ushered Davia out and gestured around the great room. "Sugar, Mari says you're to make yourself at home ri-i-ight here." Davia's ears tried to adjust to the woman's drawn-out way of talking. She still wondered where her bed was. Since linens, a pillow, and a blanket were already stacked on the couch, though, she guessed it probably opened up.

The stable was pretty ordinary on the inside, Davia thought. Just a remodeled two-bedroom apartment, clean and blah. She wondered what the insides of the *garçonnière* and the spooky-looking big house were like. Maybe no big deal, either. Maybe the only scary thing around here was her dying aunt. Where did Aunt Mari sleep? Close to Mom and Dad, Davia hoped, not close to her.

As long as I keep busy and out of the heat, she told herself, I'll be okay. So while Mom got the update from the hospice lady, Davia kept busy, busy, busy setting out food, water, and a litter box for GG, who was still cowering in her open crate. She unpacked her suitcase and stuffed her clothes willy-nilly into an empty chest. Finally, she figured out how to open the sleeper-sofa and made up the bed.

Still, she couldn't help overhearing. Mom and Sara were reading through a notebook, a sort of "bible" of everything they'd need to know—phone numbers for hospice, the nurse, the social worker, the bath aide, the chaplain—plus a journal of Aunt Mari's daily care: What she ate, when she ate, how well she ate—if she ate—and pooped and peed and slept. Same thing for her medicines, including when her next pain pill was due. Any prescriptions would be delivered by the hospice pharmacy, even in the middle of the night. "No worries," Sara assured Mom. But this was all definitely more than Davia wanted to know. Or think about.

"Davia, sweetie, aren't you interested in hearing this?" Mom asked, then turned back to Sara. "My daughter wants to be a doctor someday."

"How wonderful," Sara said. "Well, she'll certainly learn a lot, helping out here. You and your husband are doing a good thing, not shuttin' her out. Too many people do, you know, and that makes kids suffer all the more. Leastways, that's my opinion."

"Well, I hope you're right," Mom said. "Davia's a very sensitive child, and she's been through so much already."

Davia's cheeks burned. Sensitive child. Why didn't Mom say it like it was: "If it wasn't for her therapist, we'd probably still have a zombie on our hands. She's afraid of everything!" But it was true that Davia wanted to be a doctor—a lot better one than the creep who'd given her and Dad the first, devastating news about Mom's illness over the phone.

Davia forced herself closer to Mom and Sara. They talked on and on, discussing schedules for the hospice nurse, the home health aide, the social worker, and other volunteers.

"I don't think she'll be needing more volunteers," Mom said, "now that we're here."

Davia opened her mouth to protest—they could use all the help they could get—but snapped it shut when Sara said, "Well, you think on it. There's nothin' says you have to go it alone. Y'all need to take care of yourselves, too, you know. That's real important for caregivers."

"Can we see Mari now?" Mom said.

Davia guessed Mom was including her in that *we*, since Dad was back in the bedroom unpacking.

"Now?" Davia's voice squeaked.

Could she really handle this? Even through all Mom's treatments, as pale and as gray as she got, Davia had never imagined her mom dying. Well, only once. But that was her fault. She quickly pushed the memory away. Except for that one time, she'd only thought of Mom as fighting, as going "through the Valley of the Shadow of Death," like the psalm said—but just going through. Somehow, it didn't seem right to meet Grandpa Henning's sister for the first time under these circumstances. It was sort of like shaking hands with a naked person when you had all your clothes on.

"She's sleeping," Sara said, "but go on in and sit with her. Be there when she wakes up."

Mom nodded, thanked Sara, and told her they'd be fine. The front door closed with a gentle click.

Davia tried to look busy again, laying her journal and books out on a bookshelf and refolding her clothes neatly this time into separate drawers. If she could have, she would've crawled into a drawer herself.

"Sweetie, you can do that later, can't you? Let's go look in on Aunt Mari."

"But—"

"Please, Davia. This won't get any easier. And I—" Mom broke off, looking at something beyond Davia's shoulder. "I don't want her to wake up and find herself alone."

Davia tried to swallow the lump in her throat, and forced herself to think of good things—how wonderful the air conditioning would feel in there, how grateful she was that Mom would be with her. Like a little kid, Davia grabbed her mother's hand. But it felt so surprisingly small and cold, it seemed as if Mom were the little kid, not Davia.

They hesitated in the doorway. Here goes nothing, Davia thought. Her heart ticked faster than the grandfather clock in the hall. Then Mom let go and went over to pull another chair up beside the bed. Davia hung back. Her aunt barely made a dent in the white sheets. Someone had slicked her greasy, gray hair back off her high forehead. It fell stringy and straight to just below her ears. In the old photos Davia had seen of her, Aunt Mari's hair was ginger-colored and piled high atop her head. How sunken her closed eyes were now! Bony sockets jutted around them. The covers rose and fell with each breath, Davia's only clue that Aunt Mari was still alive.

"It's okay, sweetie." Mom waved her closer. "There's nothing to be afraid of."

How could Mom, of all people, say that? Wasn't she terrified, seeing how she could have easily ended up? Davia finally forced herself into the room, tiptoeing so she wouldn't awaken her great-aunt. She pretended Aunt Mari was lying in a field of poppies, like in *The Wizard of Oz*, her favorite movie. Maybe she could convince herself Aunt Mari was under a spell—just sleeping, not dying.

But the brisk scent of pine cleaner smashed that idea all to pieces.

She had expected at least a bunch of IV tubes and an oxygen mask, like on *ER*, but there were no signs of medical equipment. Except for a gleaming, modern hospital bed, old dark furniture filled the room. A silver hand mirror and matching brush lay on the dresser, along with a circle of fancy perfume bottles that glittered like jewels in the afternoon sunlight. A gray crackle-glaze ginger jar adorned a separate corner. Calm down, Davia told herself. Nothing's going to happen. Not right now. You've seen people sleep before. She took her seat beside Mom, beside Aunt Mari.

They watched and waited, and Aunt Mari slept. Once she made chewing motions, and Davia thought she saw what must be dentures come loose. Were they supposed to fix them? Mom didn't seem concerned. She went to the bathroom, then Davia did, just for something to do. When she checked on GG, all that crazy cat did was huddle up and peer at her through the little slats in the side of her crate. Once GG's pill wore off, Davia would probably never see her. Dad was reading the hospice packet out in the great room. Davia wished she could sit with him. But that wouldn't be fair to Mom, would it?

Back in Aunt Mari's room, she couldn't bear to watch the old woman just lie there and breathe anymore. She couldn't sit there doing nothing, like Mom was. How could Mom stand it? What was she thinking about? Her own cancer? Maybe she was meditating again. Davia wanted to dive back into *The Secret of Stony Manor*, but she doubted she'd be able to concentrate.

She fidgeted in her chair, and finally turned toward the window. The *garçonnière*, dark with shadows, filled the frame. She wondered whether it was air-conditioned, too. What a great place it would be for hanging out. Not that she had anyone to hang with.

Dad cleared his throat from the doorway. "I think I have just enough strength left to pick up some food." He paused. "Pick up? Get it?"

Mom groaned, shook her head.

"Do you want to come, Davia? Vacherie's not all that far. Half an hour, tops."

What if Aunt Mari woke up when they were gone? Maybe Mom would need her help. "No, thanks," she told him.

"Well, don't go anywhere without me, then," he teased.

"Like we could," Davia said, staring again at the *garçonnière*.

"What's so interesting out there?" Mom asked after Dad had gone.

Davia shrugged. How cool it would be to make the *garçonnière* her own special place! Those shutters looked like the ones on her old dollhouse. She squinted, shielding her eyes from a blinding light that reflected off the upstairs windows.

What was up with that? It couldn't be the sun. It hadn't set yet, but it was hanging low. And in the wrong direction, too.

She blinked hard, but the fierce glare persisted. Even the *garçonnière*'s arched windows on the main floor seemed to glow. She got up, faced the light, and felt almost as if she were being pulled toward it.

No. This was too weird. She had to stay away. But what was that strange light? Forget it, she told herself. Leave it alone. Push-pull. Push-pull. She was the Amazing Human Rubber Band again.

Was she seeing things? She had to get out of Aunt Mari's room, right away.

Chill, she told herself.

"Mom," she whispered, "is it okay if I go outside? Take a walk or something?" But even as she asked the question, a part of her hoped Mom would say no, it wasn't safe out there, away from her. Stay, Davia, she'd say. Where I can see you.

But the strange white light kept drawing Davia like a beacon. Don't be such a baby, she told herself. Go!

"Take a walk, sweetie? In this heat? Are you sure?"

No. She nodded. It wasn't like she'd be going to the swamp or anything.

"You'll bring your inhaler?"

Again, Davia nodded. It beat arguing about whether she even needed the stupid thing anymore.

Mom's teeth worked on her bottom lip. "Well, I suppose so. But stay right around here, okay? Don't wander off. And make sure you're back in"—she looked at her watch—"half an hour. How's that sound?"

"Fine. I'm just going to check out the *garçon-nière*. You can see me from the window."

Mom just waved. As Davia left the room, she glanced back at her sleeping Aunt Mari. She could have sworn she saw the old woman's dry, cracked lips edge upward in the faintest of smiles.

CHAPTER 2

GG's bell jingled, startling Davia as she reached the front door. Her hand froze on the knob, and she turned to see her cat sneaking across the great room's beige carpet. Their eyes met, and GG's widened, making them appear more black than aqua. Then she bolted under Aunt Mari's bed.

Mom looked up. "Everything okay, honey? Have you changed your mind about going out?"

Davia shook her head. "GG's hiding under the bed. Just so you know."

"Oh. Well, I don't think Aunt Mari's allergic, and, knowing GG, that cat's not about to make herself too comfortable."

Davia nodded. "Okay. I'm going now." She hesitated one more second. Maybe Mom would change her mind and call her back. "See you in half an hour."

Outside, Davia managed to move through the sludge that passed as air. How did people live here before air conditioning? Already her skin felt slick. It wouldn't be long before sweat trickled down her neck and pooled in her bra. If only she'd worn a ponytail. She checked her wrist for an elastic band. Nothing. She twisted her hair around and around, then lifted it off her neck. A couple of sticks in a dried-up flower bed caught her eye. She grabbed them, made them even, and stabbed them like chopsticks through her roll of hair. Brilliant!

As she rounded the end of Aunt Mari's apartment, the *garçonnière* rose before her, its glow as blinding as the Seul Choix Point Lighthouse beacon on Lake Michigan. If she were a ship, she would have read it as "danger" and stayed away. But the light pulled her toward it, seeming to push away her fears. She felt inexplicably drawn, like a moth willing to fly into a bug zapper to get to the light.

Why weren't her feet listening to her brain yell *Stop! Don't go!* Why was she going toward the building? It made no sense. Finally, she did stop, and she looked back. Her sandals had made crisp footprints in the dusty path. A wild thought flew through her mind: if something did happen to her, at least it would be easy to see where she'd gone.

Now only a raggedy hedge separated her from the *garçonnière*. For the first time Davia realized that the archways on the first floor didn't have any window panes at all. The room behind the arches had filled with a strange mist that reminded her of headlights bouncing off dense fog.

"Don't be stupid. There's a perfectly good explanation for this." Great. Now she was talking to herself. She hadn't even met Aunt Mari, and already she was catching her weirdness.

Davia gazed up at the second story and squinted against the glare. It sure was quiet. No bird calls, no insect songs, no anything. The whole world seemed to be holding its breath. She sure was. Then, from somewhere upstairs, came a sudden bang!

A slamming door? A rifle shot? Davia spun around toward the stable, her heart pounding in her ears.

"No-o-o-o-o-o." The word—if it was a word— sounded like wind moaning through trees. But not a leaf was moving.

Davia was, though. Double-time. Away from the *garçonnière*. But she may as well have been running through quicksand. Her chest felt tight. She drew a couple of puffs from her inhaler, but they didn't help. Aunt Mari's apartment didn't seem to get any closer. The wail grew louder.

"No-o-o-o-o. Don't go-o-o-o-o-o-o-o-o."

Who was that? Davia was wheezing now. And trembling. She had to get back to the stable. To Mom.

All at once, a strange, sweet perfume she didn't recognize made the air even thicker. It reminded her of something exotic she'd smelled at Jung's Nursery once when Dad had taken her to buy hanging baskets for Mother's Day. She sucked in the fragrance, and suddenly she could breathe easier. Then a blast of cold hit the back of her neck, racing along her bare arms and all through her body.

She looked down, and saw her feet moving. Her footprints were moving, too. They were disappearing behind her, as if someone had swept them up with an invisible broom. She flailed, swinging at nothing, at everything.

"Go away! Leave me alone!" She lunged, trying to shake off whatever had her in its icy fist.

And then, the stable door loomed before her, in-her-face huge.

"No-o-o-o-o-o. Don't go-o-o-o-o-o-o-o-o."

She had the knob. She was turning it, and it was opening. Rushing through the entrance, she slammed and locked the door. The moaning faded, but turned into something else—the sound of someone crying.

Davia leaned against the door, breathing hard. Something—someone—was out there. She had to tell her parents that Aunt Mari's plantation was haunted! Surely they could just send her to a nursing home or a hospital or something. The sooner they all got out of there, the better.

* * *

"No, Katharine. Do not bend it so far. Sixty degrees and no further." The raspy voice had a surprising snap to it. From the way Aunt Mari looked, thin and brittle as a wishbone, Davia had expected only whispers out of her. "You are not listening to me."

Davia tried to pull herself together. She was bursting to tell Mom what had just happened, but she couldn't make herself interrupt. Instead, she stood in the doorway. Mom was trying to adjust the angle of a drinking straw in a glass of some orangey-pink liquid. She was having trouble, though, because her fingers were still a bit numb from the chemo treatments. But the treatments had also saved Mom's life.

"There," her mother said. "Is that better?"

"Crank me up some more." Aunt Mari pointed out the electronic bed controls. "I need to see it."

Mom set the glass on the nightstand and raised the head of the hospital bed. It whirred to life. "How's that? High enough?"

Aunt Mari gave a brisk nod. "Now. Show me again."

Mom offered the straw.

"Almost, but not quite. Give it here." Aunt Mari's bony fingers worked the plastic, straightening it about a micrometer. Davia wondered whether her aunt had ever been a geometry teacher. If so, she was talking to the wrong student. Mom wasn't very mathematically oriented. She probably thought sixty degrees was a temperature. "There. You see? Now the pulp won't get stuck where it bends."

"Of course." Mom smiled and gave Aunt Mari the juice or whatever it was.

Davia watched the thick liquid climb slowly toward Aunt Mari's lips and wondered how long she'd been awake. Had she been bossing Mom around the whole time? Davia cleared her throat.

"Oh, sweetie." Mom held her hand out and Davia rushed in to grab it. Something familiar, real, and warm. "Come meet Aunt Mari."

The old woman looked up at Davia, her eyes as blue as washed denim. They were watery, rimmed with pink, and totally without lashes. Davia didn't know whether she should offer her other hand or a hug, so she just stood there and made herself smile.

"So you are Katharine's precious DAY-vee-uh." Was Aunt Mari making fun of her name? "I pronounced it correctly, did I not? Such an unusual name, I'd never heard it before. I did see it written on your birth announcement, I believe. And one, perhaps two letters over the years."

Mom eyed her lap, and squeezed Davia's hand once before she let it go.

"It's nice... I mean, I'm glad to meet you, Aunt Mari." She sank into the chair alongside Mom, her knees suddenly like overcooked spaghetti. "I hope you're...you know...feeling okay."

"Feeling being the operative word here, yes? That means I'm still alive."

"Uh...yes, I guess so." Davia glanced at the door, wishing Dad would walk in, his arms full of groceries, and give her an excuse to leave. Poof! She'd turn into his private kitchen slave on the spot.

Aunt Mari took another long pull on that sixty-degree straw. "Ahhh! Better. Here, Katharine." She offered the glass to Mom, who set it on the nightstand. "And don't forget to place a tissue on top."

Mom plucked one from the box, arranging it just so over the glass.

"And wrap one around the end of the straw, too, won't you? Germs, you know."

"Yes, Aunt Mari," Mom said, but there was a sharpness to her words that Davia had never heard before, not even when Mom was sick. "Can I get you anything else?"

"A piano?" Aunt Mari tried to smile, but her lips were too dry and cracked to move much. Davia checked the nightstand for some Vaseline, but didn't see any. She made a mental note to search the bathroom later. "Actually, there's a baby grand in the museum."

Davia frowned. "The museum?"

"You know. The Big House." Then Aunt Mari added in a whisper, "Some nights Emilie plays it."

Davia looked quickly at Mom, but couldn't tell whether she'd heard. "Who's Emilie?"

"A ghost."

"A ghost?" Davia felt her eyes grow wide.

"Aunt Mari, please." Mom turned to Davia, warning her off with a look that seemed to say, "Don't get her started."

But Davia inched to the edge of her seat anyway and leaned closer. "You're...you're kidding, right?" Considering what had just happened outside near the *garçonnière*, she had to know more. Maybe she shouldn't tell Mom after all. There was no way she'd believe her, but maybe Aunt Mari would.

"Don't 'please' me, young lady," Aunt Mari snapped, and Davia bit back a grin. Mom, at forty-seven, was hardly a young lady.

"But, Aunt Mari, we talked about this over the phone," Mom said, "didn't we? There are no such things as ghosts, here or anywhere."

"You talked, Katharine."

Mom sighed. "Yes, but I thought you...understood." She cleared her throat pointedly, then cocked her head in Davia's direction. "Honestly, Aunt Mari, I thought we agreed."

"You can stop talking about me like I wasn't here," Davia said. "At least wait till I leave the room."

"I'm sorry, Davia. I just know how you get sometimes. That imagination of yours runs wild and then you can't sleep at night." Mom slipped her arm around Davia's shoulder and squeezed. For once, Davia felt like shrugging it off. Just because she'd started back seeing her therapist again before the trip, that didn't mean she had Fragile—Handle With Care stamped on her forehead. Miss Teri had helped her see that she was stronger than she thought. When she was ready, when the time was right, she could face anything. "Honey," Mom pleaded. "I just don't want this summer to be any harder on you than it has to be."

"I wanted to come, remember?"

"Amen. Peace be with us." Aunt Mari closed her eyes and pressed her hands together like she was praying. Davia wondered whether she was being sarcastic or serious. Maybe her aunt was religious. She glanced around for a Bible or a cross or those little prayer beads, but came up empty.

"So, besides a piano," Mom said, a flicker of amusement in her eyes, "what can I get you, Aunt Mari?"

"Tea and toast would be nice. Dry, with a touch of cinnamon."

"You've got it." Mom turned to Davia; she had jumped up to help. "Do you mind staying with her, sweetie?"

Like I really have a choice. Davia stood rooted in place, chewing her bottom lip.

"You needn't worry," Aunt Mari said. "I don't bite

unless I'm ravenously hungry, and I promise I won't kick the bucket on you."

The image of Aunt Mari kicking anything on Davia, let alone a bucket, made her smile. But it freaked her out that her great-aunt had read her thoughts.

The ticking sound of a little travel clock on Aunt Mari's nightstand filled the room. Davia felt weird standing while her aunt was lying down, so she took Mom's seat beside the bed. As soon as she sat down Aunt Mari started sniffing the air, turning her head from side to side. She frowned, and then a slight smile came to her lips. "Do you smell that?" the old lady asked.

Davia sniffed nervously, but all she detected was some kind of disinfectant. And her own sweat. "No, what?"

"Gardenias." Aunt Mari jutted her chin at Davia. "You. Come closer."

Swallowing hard, Davia leaned forward. She felt her aunt's bony fingers lift the strands of hair that had fallen free of the twigs. Aunt Mari's breath was warm and moist against Davia's neck. "Just as I thought. You've met Emilie," she said, her voice surprisingly tender, like her touch.

Davia pulled away. Her aunt's eyes had a light, a fire, that she hadn't seen before. Maybe she was crazy. Really crazy. Hurry, Mom, hurry!

"Did you see any gardenias outside?" Aunt Mari asked. "Answer me. Did you?"

Davia wanted to tell her she didn't even know what a gardenia looked like, but the explanation stuck in her throat. Her aunt would think she was stupid, and she wasn't about to say every flower she'd seen out there had been dried up or dead.

"Well?" Aunt Mari snapped. "What's the matter? Did the cat get your tongue?"

Davia shook her head. She was beginning to doubt what she'd seen, what she'd smelled, what she'd felt outside near the *garçonnière*. She must have imagined the whole thing.

"Well, speak up, dear. Don't be afraid." Aunt Mari rubbed her chin, waiting.

"It's just that I..." Davia broke off, not wanting to insult Aunt Mari. "I don't know what to say, what to think. I mean, is there really a ghost here?"

Aunt Mari laid a knobby hand over Davia's. "I'm glad Emilie came to you, Davia. I sense that she needs you."

"She does?" Davia gulped.

"Yes, child. And so do I," Aunt Mari said. "We haven't much time."

CHAPTER 3

What do you mean, we don't have much time?" Davia asked. "What's going to happen?" Aunt Mari touched one finger to her lips and nodded toward the doorway.

Mom must have still been fixing a tray in the kitchen.

"Move your chair closer. You're blocking my view."

Davia did as Aunt Mari asked.

The old woman motioned her toward the pillow. Davia swallowed hard. Finally, she obeyed.

"When I die..." Aunt Mari began.

"Aunt Mari, don't say that. You've got to think positive. That's what Mom always said, and look how it helped her."

"Positive thinking or not, your mother is going to die, dear." Davia opened her mouth to protest, but Aunt Mari rushed on. "So will you. So will I. That's the way it is. The only mystery is when. Do you understand?"

She wished Aunt Mari would take back the words. True as they might be, Davia didn't want to think about that again. Her cheeks burned, and all at once, she had an overwhelming urge to stuff her face with candy, ice cream, doughnuts—anything she knew she shouldn't eat. But the words hung in the air. It was too late to unsay them.

"Do you understand?" Aunt Mari asked again.

"I don't want to," Davia whispered.

"That wasn't my question, was it?"

"No, ma'am."

"So, do you? Understand, I mean."

At last, Davia nodded weakly.

"As I was saying, when I die, everything I know about *Belle Forêt*, everything I've learned about the people who lived here—your relatives, Davia—will die with me, unless—" Aunt Mari broke off as Mom bustled in with the tea and toast.

"I'm not interrupting anything, am I?"

"Uh, no," Davia said. "Aunt Mari was just telling me about the history of this place, that's all."

"Oh, that's nice. So did you know that your great-great-great grandmother Josephine was born here?" Mom asked.

"No, Katharine, Josephine LeBlanc Ormond was *your* three-greats grandmother," Aunt Mari said. "Which makes her Davia's four-greats."

Davia's eyes crossed just thinking about their family tree. GG's pedigree chart from the Cat

Fancier's Association was hard enough to follow, and that only went back a few generations. "Wow. How do you even keep that stuff straight?"

"I've got notebooks in the *garçonnière*, if you ever want to take a look at them," Aunt Mari said.

"Cool." Maybe that would give her something interesting to do in there.

Mom set the tea and toast on a hospital tray that she wheeled over and positioned in front of Aunt Mari. Steam curled up from the mug. Davia wondered whether her aunt would have something to say about the tea being too hot or the toast being too dry.

"What are you both staring at?" Aunt Mari snapped. "Haven't you seen an old lady eat before?"

Mom released a ragged breath but said nothing. Davia wondered how long it would take before Mom blew up and gave Aunt Mari a piece of her mind. She looked longingly at the open door. Would it be okay to leave now?

GG's bells broke the awkward silence. Davia hadn't realized her cat was still under the bed. By the time she bent over to see where GG was heading, the cat had jumped up, stepped around Aunt Mari, and settled at her side beneath the hospital tray. Her seven pounds of silky grayness didn't even crease the sheets.

Aunt Mari's eyes widened as she stared down at

GG. "Oh! Oh! A cat," she gasped. "Get it off! Make it go!"

Davia snapped her fingers and made a hissing sound, knowing GG would zoom off like always. To her surprise, GG inched forward, nuzzling Aunt Mari's arm. Even as Davia moved the tray away, the cat's little paws kept kneading the covers.

"Claws! They're going to get me!"

Mom laid her arm on Aunt Mari's while Davia crossed to the other side of the bed. She couldn't believe GG still hadn't gone flying out of the room. When she picked her up, GG glared at her, and when she closed Aunt Mari's door on her, GG gave Davia a meow that sounded a lot like her own Mo-om!

"I'm sorry, Aunt Mari," Mom was saying. "She usually doesn't cotton to people. There must be something special about you she likes."

Aunt Mari scowled. Her fingers flicked at the place where GG had been. "Animals offer nothing but germs! Excrement!" She rolled her eyes up, and, through her tissue-paper skin, Davia could see a pulse pounding in her temples. "Get me up, Katharine. Put me in my chair and change the linens."

Mom turned her back on Aunt Mari for a moment. Davia bet she was counting to ten. In Swahili. *And* Catalán. When Mom turned around, she said sweetly, "Which chair? Where would you be most comfortable?"

"The wheelchair." Aunt Mari raised her chin in the direction of the attached bathroom and Davia scurried around to get the chair for her and put it beside the bed. No way did she want Aunt Mari mad at her.

Aunt Mari rasped orders out one by one—how they had to turn back the sheets; at what angle her legs needed to be; how they were supposed to hold her, scoot her, support her as she moved from the bed to the chair. Davia was going to have to ask Mom to teach her the "counting to ten in hard languages" trick; inside she was silently screaming at Aunt Mari in English and French.

Her aunt's pale pink nightgown fell like a tent from her shoulders. An orange plastic band hung loose around one bony wrist. There was some kind of typing on it—her name, maybe—and in bigger letters, DNR, whatever that meant. When the old woman moved, Davia could hear the crunch and whisper of paper and plastic.

"No need to avert your eyes, Davia." Aunt Mari had caught her standing there, gawking at her legs. They were thin as twigs and covered with scales like pale bark. "I have no modesty. No shame. Cancer takes all that."

"Yes. I remember." Mom's eyes met Davia's, then looked away. She bent over Aunt Mari, who was in the wheelchair now. "Are you warm enough? Do you want a robe?"

Aunt Mari nodded. She dragged one hand over her hair, but it still fell in gray strings. "The chenille one. Hanging up in there." She pointed across the room.

Davia entered the walk-in closet, hoping there'd be only one robe so she wouldn't have to ask what chenille was. Aunt Mari had organized her clothes—mostly old-fashioned two-piece suits and a few dresses with white collars—by color and covered them with plastic bags. They hissed together as cool air from the floor vent hit them. The smell of cedar and mothballs clung to everything. "What color is it?" she called.

"She says 'periwinkle,'" Mom called back.

Davia found the nubby bathrobe between the blues and purples. Mom draped it over Aunt Mari's thin shoulders. The way she pulled each arm through in turn reminded Davia of the time she helped dress the skeleton in science class as a Halloween prank.

"There, now. I'll go take care of these sheets." Mom stripped the bed and left.

Davia wished she could have been the one to go. Maybe Aunt Mari needed her to pass on the history of the place—if that's what she'd been hinting at—but Davia wasn't sure she wanted to find out why this so-called ghost needed her, too.

"What are you doing way over there?" Aunt Mari asked.

Davia forced herself forward and sat facing the wheelchair.

"Look. I know you don't believe in ghosts, Davia. Not many people do."

Davia opened her mouth to protest, but Aunt Mari raised a finger in warning.

"Maybe you're even afraid."

Davia's head bobbed before she could stop it.

"That's the first step, you know. Admitting you're afraid. But where there's love," Aunt Mari said, "there can be no fear."

"You're saying I'm supposed to love a ghost?" Man, she really was crazy.

Aunt Mari tried to purse her chapped lips. "Maybe you will and maybe you won't. The point is, ghosts are people, too. Or at least, they were."

"So?"

"So, ghosts have problems, just like people do. Once you get to know—"

"I'm not getting to know a ghost," Davia said, shuddering. "Not if I can help it."

"Well, if you can get to know me," Aunt Mari said, "Emilie should be a piece of cake."

Davia decided just to play along. "Why's that?"

"Don't get me wrong. She can be difficult at times. Willful. But deep down, I do believe she has a good heart. Often, when I was in pain, she came and...well, one whiff of that gardenia took it all away."

That sounded pretty incredible. But hadn't she breathed easier when she'd inhaled the same aroma near the *garçonnière*? Davia wondered where Emilie was now. Spying on them? "What does she need me for, Aunt Mari, when she already has you?"

"I'm not entirely sure. Heaven knows, I have tried my best to help her. We have things in common, Emilie and I. She knows I feel for her, but..." Aunt Mari shrugged helplessly. "Maybe I'm too old. Or it's possible she needs something that I can't give her."

"Like what?"

"A young friend, maybe?" Aunt Mari lifted one shoulder.

"Don't look at me," Davia said.

"Well, whatever it is, it's something that will help her rest in peace," Aunt Mari said. "Isn't that what every ghost needs?"

"I guess so." Outside of book and movie ghosts, Davia didn't know if she even believed in them. Her parents had talked about the spirit living on after death, especially when Mom got sick. But the whole idea seemed so confusing now. "Is that all a ghost needs, Aunt Mari?" she asked. "To rest in peace?"

"I am not prone to telling mendacities, dear."

Why did she have to use such big words? Davia avoided the old woman's eyes.

"If you don't understand a word's meaning, then ask, Davia. There's no shame in improving one's vocabulary." She paused, probably waiting for Davia to do just that, but now Davia couldn't remember the word. "For your future reference, mendacities are lies."

Davia nodded. "So you mean that everything you're saying about ghosts...about Emilie...is true, right?"

"Precisely."

"And while I'm here, I have to deal with...believe in...this Emilie person...um, ghost?"

"Well, you do have a choice, dear. But if you don't want to be a 'fraidy cat all your life, you'd best start facing things and not run away from them."

"Like Dad." The words fell out before Davia even realized she was saying them.

"Well, well." Aunt Mari raised one almost-invisible eyebrow and smiled.

"I-I shouldn't have said that."

"Why not? Are you prone to mendacities?"

Davia hung her head. She had to be fair to Dad. He hadn't run away when Mom was sick, when she needed him most. But it sure seemed like the minute the doctors said she was in remission, he found plenty of things to keep him busy and out of the house. Did he think if he stopped running, her cancer would come back?

Suddenly, this whole weird discussion about ghosts and having to help them was sounding even crazier. Davia pressed her lips together, trying not to smile.

"Mock me not, young lady," Aunt Mari said. "Until Emilie's gone, *Belle Forêt* will always be the 'haunted plantation near Vacherie.' You think any real estate agent is going to be able to sell a place like that?"

"And why should I care about that?" Davia frowned.

"Because someday *Belle Forêt* will be yours. And don't get snippy with me, miss. I still have a pretty mean backhand."

Davia sucked in her breath. Would Aunt Mari actually slap her? "Sorry," she mumbled. Being around her aunt was like walking on eggshells. How exactly was she supposed to get rid of a ghost she didn't even believe in? If she hadn't smelled that sweet floral scent herself, she might have thought Aunt Mari was a total nutcase. "Okay, let's pretend I decide to play ghost-buster. So, like, what am I supposed to do?"

"Simply be her friend. Can you manage that?"

Friend. Funny she should mention that. Davia's own so-called friends had stopped coming around or calling when Mom got sick. Or maybe she stopped calling them back, afraid to leave her mother's side. And around *Belle Forêt*, friend-prospects were not exactly great—unless she counted a ghost. Davia managed a glum half-smile.

"I see nothing funny in my question, which you have not answered yet, I might add."

"I-I guess I could try to be her friend," Davia said at last. "If she's nice and...you know, not scary."

"I found these clean linens."

Davia jumped at the sound of Mom's voice. What expression did her mother see frozen on her face? Had she heard them talking about Emilie? Suddenly, Aunt Mari started coughing and slumped forward.

"Are you okay?" Davia bent closer, her arm around Aunt Mari's back. Each vertebra felt like a knuckle on a clenched fist.

The coughing continued, but Aunt Mari turned her face toward Davia. She winked, and Davia relaxed.

"Maybe a sip of juice." Mom offered Aunt Mari the glass.

"No, no. I'm okay. Help me up, Davia."

By the time Aunt Mari sat upright again, Mom was already making the bed and seemed to have forgotten that she'd walked in on their conversation. Davia gratefully helped her.

"Hospital corners, and make them tight." Aunt

Mari shook her finger at Davia, at the way she'd stuffed the sheet under the mattress, but Davia had no idea what she was talking about. "Don't you teach that girl anything, Katharine?"

"Not that, I guess." Mom came around to demonstrate lifting the sheet up, making a sharp angle and tucking first the bottom piece, then the top. It seemed a lot faster Davia's way. Not that she'd say so, of course.

"There. That's better."

"You must be tired," Mom said. "Let's get you back in bed."

"First, let me use the commode." Aunt Mari pointed. In the corner Davia saw the same kind of portable toilet Mom had used after chemo when she was too weak to walk to the bathroom. She remembered sliding the pot out and emptying it some mornings when Dad had to rush off early to teach a class. He'd always made her wear rubber gloves, though Davia had felt weird about that. What if Mom thought her own daughter was afraid of catching cancer from her pee?

"Do you want some help?" Mom asked now.

Aunt Mari shook her head.

"Privacy, then?"

When Aunt Mari did not reply, Mom motioned Davia toward the door. Aunt Mari struggled to her feet, then tottered toward the commode. It amazed Davia that those matchstick legs didn't snap under the weight of the rest of her, that she was still strong enough to get there on her own. Davia couldn't tear herself away. What if Aunt Mari fell?

"Come on, honey," Mom said, finally.

Out in the hall, Mom left the door open a crack, but pulled Davia away. "Tell me the truth now. Did she start in again with that ghost nonsense?"

Davia looked away. She wasn't much good at lying, and Mom and Dad had never lied to her. Especially not about Mom's illness and her slim odds of beating it—a less than five percent chance she'd live more than two years. It had already been three. Davia smiled up at Mom now, grateful she'd managed overtime. "How come Aunt Mari is so rich, anyway?" she asked, changing the subject. "How can she afford a big plantation like this?"

"She inherited it after her mother died. Actually, your Great-Grandma Rose left her two plantations. But Mari sold the Ormond place on Bayou Lafourche right away."

"Two plantations! You're kidding. Didn't Aunt Mari ever marry? Have kids?"

Mom shook her head. "It was very sad. Everyone thought at forty-four, she was too old to get married. I was only four when she met Robert, but oh, what a love story, to hear Mari tell it! They were planning a fancy outdoor wedding right here at *Belle Forêt*. But he died a few days before the big event."

"Wow." A wave of sympathy washed through Davia as she tried to picture Aunt Mari younger and in love—for maybe the first and last time. How sad was that? "What happened?"

"He had an accident. Fell from a ladder, I think, and hit his head. It happened right—" Mom broke off. "Never mind. It's not important."

Davia was still stuck on the fact that her great-aunt never had children. "So you're the only relative Aunt Mari has?"

"I think so, unless there are some distant cousins I don't know about."

Did Mom have a clue that she'd probably inherit *Belle Forêt* once Aunt Mari died? How else could *Belle Forêt* someday be Davia's, as Aunt Mari had said? Is that why her mother had decided to get back in touch with such a crotchety old lady? Davia hated to think Mom could be that way. She sighed, eyed the dust on her sandal straps, thought again about her disappearing footsteps, and shivered.

"Are you cold? Want me to adjust the air?"

"No, it's okay." She edged toward Aunt Mari's door. "Shouldn't we check on her?"

Before Mom could answer, GG shot past them into Aunt Mari's bedroom. "Uh-oh," Mom said. "Quick! Get that cat out of there before we have to change the sheets again."

Davia knocked lightly. "Aunt Mari? Okay if I come in?"

"Shoo! Scat!" she heard, then a horrible hissing sound. Davia couldn't believe GG had it in her.

"I'll get her, don't worry," she said, bursting in.

GG sat in the wheelchair, blinking over at Aunt Mari. Still on the commode, the old woman had pulled her lips back, baring her teeth. And Davia realized, to her amazement, that it was Aunt Mari, not GG, who was hissing so fiercely. But that crazy cat seemed to have gone deaf. She slunk down in the chair, her chin on her paws, waiting out Aunt Mari's hissy fit.

Why did GG insist on approaching people who didn't want her—and avoid the ones who did? Davia would never figure that cat out.

"GG, go!" Davia clapped her hands. When the cat didn't move, she picked her up and handed her off to Mom. They looked at each other in disbelief. "Maybe we should put her back in the crate," Davia said. "For now, anyway."

"I'll take her," Mom said.

Once they were alone again, Aunt Mari told Davia how to disinfect her wheelchair, step by step. Pine cleaner. That was her big thing. She insisted that Davia put on rubber gloves from the bathroom—hospice had supplied a whole box—and use the stuff straight from the bottle. The room reeked, and Davia's nose itched. By the time she'd helped her aunt toddle over to the now germ-free wheelchair, Mom was back.

"Did you lock that little beast up, Katharine?"

"Yes, Aunt Mari."

"I-I'm sorry. I don't know what's gotten into her," Davia said, as they eased Aunt Mari into bed again. "She usually hides from everybody."

"I don't suppose it's my animal magnetism." Aunt Mari tried to wink at Davia, but instead squeezed both eyes shut for a moment. She drew in a breath through clenched teeth. Her fingers clutched at the sheets Davia had just pulled up to her chin.

Mom glanced at her watch. "It's almost time for your pill, Aunt Mari. Let me go check the book to make sure."

Aunt Mari nodded and finally looked up at Davia. "I'm such a bother. I'm sorry. You and your parents have better things to do than sit around waiting for a bossy old lady to give up the ghost."

"What?" Davia asked. Was she talking about Emilie again?

"Give up the ghost?" Aunt Mari laughed lightly. "It's another way to say die. Not that I ever dwell on the word, but..." She offered a tight, painful-looking smile. "I truly am grateful y'all came down here. I want you to know that."

"We know." Aunt Mari's heartfelt thanks took Davia aback. Her eyes welled unexpectedly. "Hey, let me get you something for those chapped lips." She rummaged through the bathroom and when she came back with the Vaseline, Mom was giving Aunt Mari a sip of juice to wash down her pill. Davia wondered whether it would make her sleepy. Would Emilie visit Aunt Mari as soon as they left her room? Were there other ghosts hanging around that Aunt Mari hadn't mentioned?

There were so many things she didn't know, Davia realized. The big question was, did she really want to?

CHAPTER 4

T hat night the sound of hissing awoke Davia, and she remembered Aunt Mari's standoff with GG. She rubbed her eyes, then looked around, trying to figure out where her cat was. A full moon streamed into her room, past the open drapes. She had insisted they be left open because Mom couldn't persuade Aunt Mari to part with one of the bazillion nightlights in her room. Dad had promised to get Davia her own supply the next time he ran errands.

Now GG stood silhouetted on the window ledge, her back arched, her tail stiff and unusually full. She was hissing, almost growling, at something outside.

"GG, what is it, girl?" Davia pushed the covers aside, rolled out of bed, and tiptoed toward the window. Though she expected GG to race away as she got closer, the gray cat stood there, each hair quivering, showing her teeth. "What do you see, huh?"

Davia looked past their car, beyond the dirt lane. Mosquitoes swarmed everywhere. Some kind of fog hung over the lawn, shimmering in the moonlight. It reminded her of what she'd seen earlier in the *garçonnière*. She blinked and rubbed her eyes again, trying to see what GG saw. But her vision still seemed wrapped in sleep.

Now the hissing turned to spitting. Davia laid her hand on the cat's back and managed to stroke all the way to the tip of her tail before GG shot off the ledge and darted under the bed. With a sigh, Davia watched her go, then turned back to the window. And though her hands were trembling, her curiosity worked overtime.

The fog had resettled in one place like a cloud-puff in a hollow. As she watched, it turned into something. A girl! Davia gasped and took a step back from the window.

The girl waltzed toward Davia, dark ringlets and long white skirt swaying. She seemed to walk right through their car, and as she approached the window, Davia saw a white flower with glossy green leaves in her hair. The strange girl's face reminded her of Grandma Henning's cameo, only sadder.

"Emilie?" Davia whispered. She didn't expect an answer. Still, something seemed to be pulling the girl toward her. The closer she came, the more she looked like Davia's own reflection—only Davia was wearing a cotton nightgown and the girl was wearing a lace dress that swept the ground, and maybe petticoats, too.

Davia's stomach knotted. A ghost! Goose bumps raced down her arms. Despite the air conditioning, a tightness started in her chest, followed by a whistling sound when she breathed in. She fumbled through her purse for her inhaler and took a couple of puffs, but they didn't help. In her mind, she and her parents were already racing to the emergency room.

"Mom!" she thought she screamed, but the words must not have escaped. No one came. Her feet felt melted into the carpet. Then she remembered the gardenia smell—how strangely it had affected her before, by the *garçonnière*. How much easier it had been to breathe. She opened the window toward the ghost, only a crack. When she tried to speak, her voice still wouldn't come. But a whiff of gardenia did, and one deep breath worked like heavy-duty meds. Amazing.

The girl reached out to Davia with open arms, as if she wanted to give her a hug. Or grab her up and drag her away. Davia recoiled and stepped back from the window. She thought of all the ghost stories she'd ever read, how those ghosts sometimes seemed nice and friendly. But often they weren't. If this was Emilie, Aunt Mari had trusted her, and now Aunt Mari was dying.

Davia looked away, glancing around the room.

Surely she'd be safe inside with her parents sleeping in the next room. What if she opened the window farther? Would the girl talk to her? Ghosts did talk, didn't they? Her heart hammered at the thought. It drowned out the little voice that kept saying, "Don't do anything stupid." She cranked the window another couple of inches and touched her fingers to the screen.

The ghost-girl drifted closer. "Who are you, please?" She had a trace of an accent—French, maybe—and her voice sounded all echo-y, like it was traveling to Davia through a cave. "What business have you here, at *Belle Forêt*?"

Davia couldn't move, couldn't say a word.

"You do speak English, yes?"

She nodded, still stunned that a ghost was talking. To her.

"Then speak!"

Who does she think she is, ordering me around? Davia glanced back at her bed, wishing GG had never awakened her. Then this could all be a dream.

"This is my home and I did not invite you," the ghost-girl said. "At least tell me your name."

"I-it's...Davia," she managed, finally. "And my...my aunt owns this place. She invited me."

"Mari? She is your aunt?"

"My great-aunt." Davia blew out a quick breath. "A-are you going to tell me your name?"

"Emilie LeBlanc."

So now Emilie had a last name, too. The same as Davia's four-greats grandmother Josephine. She let that sink in. "Aunt Mari told me about you. She's dying."

Emilie cocked her head as if she didn't believe Davia. "Her body may die. But her spirit, *non!* More important, she will rest in peace."

Davia eyed her bare feet, remembering how Aunt Mari had said the same thing about Emilie. But what did Emilie want with her, Davia? Again, she rubbed her eyes. Maybe when she opened them, Emilie would be gone and this would all have been her imagination.

"Mari says you have to be my friend."

Davia's eyes snapped open. "That is not what she said. And I don't have to be anything. You're not the boss of me, and neither is she." Whoa. Where did that come from? How stupid to risk ticking off a ghost she didn't really know anything about!

"Touché!" Emilie clapped her hands and gave a quick curtsy. "You want to fight? *Eh, bien.* I should like to tame that spirit of yours."

Davia gulped. She wondered what Emilie meant, and didn't know what to say.

"It is good you are here with Mari. I swear to you, no one should die alone."

"My dad is here. And my mom, too. Just so you know."

Emilie laughed. "Look at you, all puffed up like a peacock! You think they will keep you safe? *Non.* My parents did not, I tell you that. In the end, we have only ourselves to rely on."

"I don't believe you," Davia said. "And I don't have to listen to you, either." She turned to go, but realized she'd forgotten to close the window. As if a closed window could keep out a ghost. Couldn't they go wherever they wanted, when they wanted? Maybe she should have tried harder to be nice.

"*Non!* Wait! I implore you. Let me apologize, please. We...we did not begin well. You must permit me to try again."

Davia blew out a long breath and turned around. As she did, a cloud passed over the moon. In the sudden darkness, Emilie looked less like an innocent girl dressed in white and more like a ghost in a black shroud. Pure evil. Davia shrank from the sight. She backed up, swallowing hard, until her calves hit the metal frame of the sofa-bed.

"No-o-o-o-o-o. Don't go-o-o-o-o-o-o." Emilie's wail filled Davia's ears. Maybe it would awaken her parents!

Davia scrambled into bed. Sleep. She had to go back to sleep and lose herself in a dream. Maybe when she woke up, she would forget that any of this had happened. As she pulled the covers over her head, she felt GG snuggle under them and into the curve of her waist. Davia held her breath, amazed at the miracle of the tiny warm body willingly pressed against hers. Though at first her heartbeat thrummed in her ears, with each passing moment she felt heavier and heavier.

***

Davia squinted as she stood near the great room window, trying to make out the ghost-girl through a dense white fog. At last, Emilie emerged from the mist.

"*Bonjour.* My name is Emilie LeBlanc. It would please me if we could be friends."

There. That's better, Davia thought. I'm dreaming now, right? "I-I don't know about the friend part," she replied. "But I promise, if you're nice to me, I'll be nice to you. Okay?"

"Fair enough."

Only in her imagination would she be talking so casually to a ghost. Davia shifted her weight from one foot to the other. Maybe she should turn the conversation to Aunt Mari. That seemed safe enough, something they had in common. "I guess you've known my aunt for a long time, but I haven't. I just met her. And now she's going to die. I just wish I weren't so...scared."

"Of me, Davia?"

"No. Of course not," she said, too quickly. Did that sound convincing? "Scared for Aunt Mari."

"*Oui*. How well I know that feeling. I watched my own brother die—my beloved Michel—and the *bébés*, too. My infant sisters. If only I had lived to be a doctor—" Emilie broke off. "Well. Who knows how many people I could have cured?"

"You wanted to be a doctor? Really?" Did they even let women become doctors back then, whenever it was?

Davia turned this coincidence over in her mind. And that wasn't the only one. She and Emilie looked like they could have been sisters, too. Considering the way they'd been talking, they could have even been friends. This must be a dream, Davia thought. How else could she have given Emilie an instant personality makeover?

"A doctor, *absolument!*" Emilie rushed on, breathless. "This I have wanted with all my heart, ever since I had ten years. Do you know who Elizabeth Blackwell is? I mean, was?"

Davia shook her head.

"She became the first woman doctor in America in 1849. My brother, he told me of her. That is why I convinced my *maman* to permit me to learn English, so I could travel north and study medicine, exactly like Dr. Blackwell."

"Cool. I want to be a doctor, too," Davia admitted. "Maybe. If I can stop being so afraid of..." She couldn't say death. Not when she was talking through the window to the ghost of someone who'd probably been dead for over a hundred years. Maybe over a hundred and fifty. "...afraid of, well, everything."

"Silly goose." When Emilie smiled, she seemed almost human. "You only think you are afraid. Look. You are talking to a ghost now, are you not?"

"I guess so." Davia supposed dreaming made it easier to drop her guard.

"So much we have in common, Davia. Do you speak French?"

"Sort of." The question surprised her and she didn't want to brag. But she hadn't won Wingra Country Day School's French medal twice for nothing.

"Good." The ghost-girl beckoned with a delicate white finger. "Come with me to the Big House."

"I don't think that's such a good idea."

Emilie pouted. "You do not trust me?"

"No offense." Davia thought fast. "I wouldn't go anywhere with anyone I just met."

"So suspicious you are. It is just a visit."

"We're visiting right now. What's the big deal?"

"In the Big House, we must converse only in French. Even after all these years, I still try to honor my parents' wishes, like a good Creole daughter."

"Yeah, well, we can talk French here, too."

"Davia, do not be difficult. Mari has preserved everything exactly as it was when I was in my earthly body. Surely you wish to admire her work."

Maybe the mansion *was* like a museum inside. But the outside looked anything but preserved. Davia hesitated. Was this a trick?

"So, you will come, then?" Emilie held out her hand.

"Now?" Davia's mouth went dry. "I, uh..." She bit her lip and glanced over her shoulder, half-expecting—or maybe half-wishing—that Mom or Dad would be standing there, listening to her talk to...who? Herself is what they'd think, unless they could see Emilie, too. In that case, she imagined them and Emilie having a real tug-of-war over her. She knew her parents would win. No contest. This was still her dream, right? Couldn't she just keep talking to Emilie through the window?

"Please, Davia."

She tried on the idea, but once again rejected the thought of trusting a ghost. It was too crazy. And if that wasn't reason enough to say no, she pictured Mom's face—and Dad's—if they woke up and found her gone. "I-I can't, Emilie. Not now. Not in the middle of the night." Great. Now Emilie would invite her in the middle of the day.

"You will say yes, my friend. I always get what I want."

Now Emilie seemed more spoiled brat than friend. Davia pressed her lips together and fumed silently. "Maybe that's true," she said at last, "but you can't always get it when you want it."

"*Eh bien*, Davia. You will see. *Au revoir*." In the silver moonlight, Emilie's white dress swirled out and around. Then she disappeared into the fog.

Fine. Go. See if I care. In her dream, Davia was cranking the window closed when she heard a low moan. Okay, Emilie. Cut the drama. Still she listened, her heart beating fast. The moan came again, closer this time. Not Emilie, she decided. Maybe it was GG.

But when Davia reached for the cat, she realized that she herself was actually standing, no longer lying in bed. The covers had been flung aside. Her pillow had fallen to the floor. So she hadn't been dreaming? This long, almost-normal conversation with Emilie—had it really happened?

She shook her head and blinked hard, trying to get her bearings and make sense of it. Maybe she'd been walking and talking in her sleep. What other explanation could there be? Was Emilie still outside? She scanned the lawn, where she had first seen her. But the ghost-girl was gone.

Still, the groaning continued. Surely Emilie hadn't entered the stable! Davia realized now that the sound was coming from behind Aunt Mari's closed door.

Careful to keep GG out, Davia rushed to her aunt's side. Nightlights glowed about the room like fireflies. She doubted Aunt Mari would have missed one once she fell asleep.

"Aunt Mari, it's Davia," she whispered. "Are you okay?"

The old woman moaned again and sucked in air between her teeth. In the faint light, Davia saw her face twist in pain.

"I'll get Mom." She started to go, but Aunt Mari's bony hand caught her wrist. The strength of the grip took her aback. She wanted to shake it off, pry herself loose. "What is it?" she whispered instead.

Aunt Mari's lips pursed, then went slack again. She did this several times and Davia wondered whether she was having trouble with her dentures—or trying to speak. She bent closer, her ear near the old woman's mouth. "So many *bébés*..." Aunt Mari murmured. "Fever."

Finally, Davia uncurled Aunt Mari's fingers from around her wrist. The thought struck her: Why should I be afraid of a living person when I was just with a ghost? She softened toward the old woman then, and stroked Aunt Mari's arm. It lay limp now on the covers. Her hand freed, she placed it on Aunt Mari's forehead as Mom had done to her a bazillion times. She was no expert, but it didn't feel hot. "Aunt Mari, wake up. You're having a bad dream."

In the dim light, Davia couldn't tell whether Aunt Mari's eyes were open as she struggled to sit up. When she didn't succeed, she motioned Davia closer. "No, not a dream," she whispered. "It's true. It happened."

"What? What happened?"

She looked at Davia blankly then, as if she couldn't quite remember.

"You said something about *bébés*. And fever." In Davia's dream-that-wasn't-a-dream, Emilie had said something about *bébés*, too.

Aunt Mari winced at another stab of pain.

Davia's chest went tight. "You need a pill," she said. "I'm getting Mom."

Her mother didn't wake easily, though. Davia wondered whether she'd taken one of her old sleeping pills from when she was sick, or whether she was just plain exhausted after their long first day with Aunt Mari. Dad mumbled something and rolled over. When Mom finally sat up, her curls were matted down on one side, making her head look lopsided. As she put some slippers on—hard-bottomed ones so she wouldn't lose her balance—Davia steadied her.

"You look so tired, Mom," she said. "I'm sorry I woke you, but Aunt Mari's—"

"Don't be silly. I'm fine, sweetie." But something in her voice made Davia stick closer. Was Mom sick again? How would they know if she was?

Together they checked the notebook, and Mom gave Aunt Mari some medicine. Then she sat on the bed, stroking Aunt Mari's hair back off her forehead.

"Fever," Aunt Mari whispered.

"No, you feel cool." Davia heard the smile in Mom's voice. "Just try to relax now. I'm here. Davia and I are here. You're not alone." She turned to Davia. "Thanks for getting me. You go on to bed now. I'll sit with her."

"Are you sure?"

"I'm fine."

"Okay, okay." Davia backed off, wounded by the slap in Mom's tone. But in a way, she was glad to go. She wanted to think about her first face-to-face meetings with Emilie. She doubted they would be her last. "Good night, Aunt Mari. See you in the morning."

Alone in the great room, she tried to convince herself Mom really was okay. *She'd said that before, and I believed her.* Davia pushed the thought away and wished suddenly that Emilie would come back. Was she so starved for company she'd actually look forward to being with a ghost?

Pressing her face to the window, she searched for Emilie, but the ghost-girl had not returned. The mist had lifted, painting the lawn with dew. It was strange that both Emilie and Aunt Mari had used the same word—*bébés*. Not babies. But *bébés*. French. The word rang in Davia's ears.

With a sigh, she drew the drapes, crawled back into bed, and pulled up the covers. For once, dark-ness seemed more like a cozy blanket than something to be feared. She'd have to remember to tell Dad to cross nightlights off his To Do list. Before long, she heard Aunt Mari's door close softly and smelled Mom's vanilla night cream in the dark. When her mother sat on the edge of the hide-a-bed, Davia rolled toward her.

"Long day," Mom said. "I'm not used to waiting on someone so..."

"Yeah, I know what you mean."

"I guess I was really out of it. I'm sorry she woke you."

"She didn't," Davia said. "I was awake."

"Something on your mind?"

"No."

"Bed uncomfortable?"

"Uh-huh."

"We'll see what we can do about that tomorrow, okay?" Mom's hand felt cool on Davia's forehead. "Try to get some sleep now."

"Is Aunt Mari all right?"

Mom didn't answer at first, but when she did, her voice sounded strange, far away. "She's dying, honey." Davia wondered whether her mother was remembering her own brush with death.

"Never mind," Davia whispered, but she found Mom's hand in the darkness and held it tight.

"Well...anyway." Mom sighed. Davia listened hard for something more than tiredness. After all that chemo, was tired just normal? "Try to get some sleep, Davia."

"Okay."

"Your dad's going to sit with Aunt Mari in the morning and give us a break. Maybe the two of us can go for a walk."

"That'd be great. No offense to Aunt Mari."

"None taken," Mom said. "I'm sure she's going to die the way she lived—obsessive and fussy to the end."

"So she was always like that?"

"Yes. And it served her well all those years as a research librarian at Tulane. I got to know her better when Dad and I were students there. My father died then, and Aunt Mari and I, we sort of helped each other through it."

"I'm sorry, Mom."

"Yeah, that was a hard time for both of us. But Aunt Mari had a flat in the Garden District, and she had us over there a lot."

"Did you ever come here? She must have owned *Belle Forêt* then, right?"

Mom nodded. "Yes, but she never lived here until after Dad and I graduated. She took an early retirement, said she wanted to be closer to Robert's spirit." Mom sighed. "I still don't know what made her decide to do that. By then, he'd been dead for, what? Twenty years?"

"Weird. We'll have to ask her." It sounded like

Aunt Mari had believed in ghosts even back then. Davia tried to stifle a yawn. She didn't want Mom to think she wasn't interested in what she was saying, because she was. More than Mom knew.

"Sorry, sweetie, I'm rambling. I should let you get some sleep."

Davia nodded and let the yawn come. "Night."

Mom kissed her cheek, touched her hair. She seemed okay now. Davia closed her eyes.

CHAPTER 5

The next morning, only Dad was at the breakfast table. He'd set out spoons, bowls, and bananas, along with a box of cereal—his boring healthy kind—and a carton of milk.

"Where's Mom?" Davia asked.

"She's coming."

Right away, Davia began to worry again. "Is she okay?"

Dad nodded, but Davia didn't believe him. Ever since the doctor had said her mother was in remission, Mom had made it a point to get up early. "Don't want to waste precious time sleeping in," she'd joked. Davia had come to expect her happy face first thing in the morning, making them all glad for a new day together.

"Are you sure, Dad?"

"Honestly, Davia, she's fine. Said she wasn't hungry, that's all. She's probably just pooped after waiting on Aunt Mari hand and foot. Let's not make a federal case out of it."

She watched him slice a banana into his bowl. *Plop. Plop. Plop.* Like everything was normal. She wished she could believe him. She couldn't wait for Dad to watch Aunt Mari so she and Mom could get out of here for a while.

"Come on, sit down and eat. You're a growing girl."

"Don't remind me."

"No need to be touchy. I didn't mean it that way, honey."

"No. You were just joking, right?" She was sick to pieces of him covering everything up with puns. And not the greatest ones, at that. Still, she hadn't meant to hurt his feelings. Somewhere beneath all those jokes, she was sure he still had some.

He stared at those bananas for the longest time. Davia sat down beside him.

"This is all very hard for you, isn't it?" Dad said. "Seeing Aunt Mari just brings everything back about Mom's...illness."

Davia didn't answer.

"For me, too, you know. Probably for your mom as well."

Davia picked at another hangnail until it bled.

"I honestly think you'd be better off at camp, no matter what Miss Teri says."

"I'm better off with Mom. Believe me, Dad."

"Your mother's got a good attitude, you know. Full speed ahead. Make every day count. No looking back. No worrying about the future."

"She worries plenty about *my* future."

"Well, that's her job. She's a mother," he said.

"Da-ad."

"I know. She does go overboard sometimes." His sigh seemed to fill the whole room. "But we could learn from her, you and I. She's given us a real gift."

"A gift?"

"The Present." His dimples showed, even though he hadn't shaved yet.

"I don't get it," Davia said.

Dad sighed again. "It's a play on words, Davia. Gift? Present? But I'm serious. You...we...need to do more of that, more living in the Now. The past, the future, they don't really exist. And worrying about them only spoils the one thing we do have. Today."

She tried to let his words sink in, but they were like rain splatting on blacktop. "It's not that easy," she said finally, and poured herself some cereal. "You still worry, too."

"I never said it was easy, D. Just that we ought to try harder to live that way."

When Mom came out of the bedroom at last, Davia couldn't stop staring at how great she looked.

She'd put on makeup, and she was wearing a new outfit. Both brought out the glint in her pale green eyes. Davia felt like kicking herself. Why couldn't she even let Mom be tired without worrying? Her mother was holding a pair of manicure scissors in one hand and trying to twist around to cut off two dangling price tags.

"Here," Davia said, jumping up and putting her bowl in the sink. "Let me help."

"You're still going to stay with Mari, right, Ken?"

Dad nodded.

"Thanks," Mom said. "We won't go far."

The minute they stepped outside into the hot thick air, Davia knew they wouldn't be gone long, either. Still trying to get used to the humidity, she was moving in slow motion. Mom wasn't in any rush, either. They'd barely made it out the door when her mother patted the back pocket of Davia's shorts.

Yes, I listened to you, Mom. Yes, I brought my inhaler. A little voice inside her head whispered, "Quit it, Mom," but Davia ignored it and let it go. She reminded herself of Mom's latest favorite expression: Don't sweat the small stuff. She'd rather have Mom here to worry about her and drive her crazy than not have her here at all.

"Feels like a storm's coming," Mom said. "Maybe some rain will cool things down."

Davia looked up, squinting. Was a yellow pea-soup sky a sign of rain down South? "So, where do you want to go?" she asked.

Mom's face lit up like a little kid emptying her trick-or-treating pillowcase for the first time. "You know what I've always wanted to see? The Big House."

Davia immediately thought of Emilie and how she'd wanted her to go there last night. She shivered. Where did Emilie hang out in the daytime?

"I can't wait to see all the antiques inside," Mom went on. "They're supposed to be really amazing. I wonder if Aunt Mari will leave everything to the historical society."

Davia hesitated. "Actually, she kind of told me she's leaving it to you."

"Me? You're kidding." Mom looked stunned. "I mean, surely there are cousins or..." Her voice trailed off. "Sorry. I guess I just won't believe it unless Aunt Mari tells me herself."

"Well, I wouldn't use...mendacities."

Mom raised her faint eyebrows. "No, of course not, honey. That's not what I meant." She shook her head. "What on earth would we do with a plantation?"

Davia shrugged. "Maybe someday you could make it into a bed and breakfast."

Mom laughed. "Oh, yes. I can just see myself

slaving away in the kitchen and your father making beds."

Davia giggled. "Okay, forget that idea." The day Mom loved to cook and Dad loved to wait on people would probably coincide with the End of the World.

They walked across the lawn where Davia had first seen Emilie. She glanced around nervously. Surely Emilie wouldn't come waltzing up to them in broad daylight—especially not with Mom here. She felt herself relax a bit.

The grounds looked as neglected as the outside of the Big House, and the grass was sorely in need of cutting. "I could do the lawn," Davia said. "Maybe Aunt Mari has a mower."

Mom smiled. "I think we'll give that chore to your father. All that grass—it's not good for your allergies."

Davia just sighed. Leave it to Mom to invent new reasons to worry. That's her job, Dad had said. She shook her head. It was amazing Mom even let her wash dishes. She might break a nail—or break out in hives from the dish soap.

A path curved around rosebush skeletons and led to the alley of massive oak trees on their left and the Big House on their right. Davia had forgotten how high the mansion sat off the ground, raised up on those sturdy brick stilts. She and Mom could walk under there without hitting their heads, but Dad would probably have to duck. Davia made her way around the staircase and took a few steps into the gloomy, open-air basement-like place beneath the house.

"Where are you going?" Mom asked.

"Nowhere." Davia kept inching forward, though, and suddenly it felt as if she had stepped inside a walk-in refrigerator, the kind they had at camp. "Hey, check this out!"

"Come out of there, Davia. It doesn't look safe."

Davia squinted into the darkness, and sniffed the air. No scent of gardenias, which probably meant no Emilie. Good. How dangerous could it be?

"Watch out for snakes," Mom said, in an off-handed way that made Davia wonder whether she was joking or being serious.

"You're kidding, right?"

"I'm not. That's the worst thing about the South—super-poisonous snakes."

Snakes! Davia beat a hasty retreat from the crisp air, back into the stifling heat.

"Thank you," Mom said. She gave Davia the same brave little smile she'd given the chemo nurses.

"Well, where to next?" Davia asked.

"Race you to the top of the stairs!" Mom sang out, and her sandals slapped the sagging planks.

But Davia didn't have the energy. "You win," she called from near the bottom.

Mom grinned down at her and made a V in the air with her arms. It reminded Davia of the last big trip they'd taken, before Mom got sick, to Mexico— and how Mom had stood on top of the Great Pyramid at Chichén Itzá. Dad had talked her into going all the way up, step by narrow step. But when Davia saw people crawling down backward on their hands and knees because there were no handrails, she'd chickened out and waited on the ground, watching them go. But she loved how triumphant Mom had looked, in the middle of all that sky.

"Come on!" Mom waved her up.

Davia puffed her way to the top of the stairs. Huge pillars supported the overhang from the roof that shaded them. A porch encircled the house. There were tall floor-to-ceiling windows on each side of two double-wide front doors. Padlocked chains held them closed.

"Now what?" Davia asked, wondering how Emilie had expected her to come inside. She wasn't exactly a magician.

Mom frowned, shook her head. "Padlocks! I should have known. Even out here in the middle of nowhere."

Hey. You noticed. Internet and cable TV would have been nice. Davia shrugged. "I'm sure she has her reasons."

"I suppose." Mom approached one of the windows and shielded her eyes, trying to see inside.

Davia tried, too, but a gauzy white curtain blocked her view. Her reflection bounced back at her, with her eyes like dark holes. "Let's go all the way around," she suggested. "Maybe some of the windows don't have curtains."

"And maybe some aren't latched."

"Dream on, Mom."

They started around the Big House, peeking at each window, trying to raise the sash. But the rotting wood held firm. Davia sensed dark furniture and rich colors beyond the film of white. Was Emilie nearby? She breathed deeply, checking for a trace of gardenia. But dust and mold were all she smelled. "Think Aunt Mari would give us the keys?" she asked, finally.

"Can't hurt to ask. I'm dying to see what she's done inside. Once she moved here, she was determined to bring this place back to its former glory."

"I wonder why she let the outside go," Davia said. Even a blind person could tell it needed paint and new windows. They could have been the originals, for all she knew.

As Davia and Mom made their way along one side of the porch, it bowed and groaned beneath their feet. They rounded the corner to the back of the house, the part closest to the stable. But the doors on that side, too, were locked with chains.

Mom shook her head and sighed. "Well, that was exciting. Come on, sweetie, let's go."

"One more minute." Davia kept checking each window on the final side of the house.

"Don't bother." Mom studied the sky. "Let's get back before it rains."

Still, Davia dawdled. The last window threw her reflection back at her. But how could her hair be long and loose around her face, when she was sure she'd put it up in a ponytail? She shook her head, felt her hair swish against her neck. But the face in the window did not move. Was it Emilie's? "Mom! Check this out! Quick!"

"What's up?" Her mother's voice came from a long way off. When Davia looked, Mom had already reached the bottom of the stairs. She was leaning over, examining something on the ground. A single muffled, angry word floated up to Davia through the hot, thick air.

"Mom, are you okay?"

"Just stubbed my toe, that's all."

"Is it bleeding?"

"Yep."

"Lots?"

"I won't need a transfusion, sweetie."

Transfusion. Davia's mind clamped down on the word. She talked herself back to the present. The Now. "Don't joke about that, Mom. It's not funny."

"I wasn't trying to be." Mom fished a tissue out

of her pocket and wrapped it around her big toe. "What did you want, anyway? Did you see some furniture?"

"No," Davia called, "but—"

"Come on, honey. Let's go back. Next time we'll ask Aunt Mari for the keys."

"I'll be down in a sec." Davia turned to go, but couldn't. Not yet. Not till she'd checked out that reflection.

When she glanced back at the window, though, the face was gone. Frustrated, she was turning to leave when something strange caught her eye. Scratches in the glass pane. Big, wavery letters that seemed to teeter above the sill.

She frowned, peering closer, and finally ran her finger over the dusty window. IOM-ZEVUAS. On the inside of the glass. She flipped the letters around to make them read correctly in her mind's eye—SAUVEZ-MOI.

Davia froze. She knew what the French words meant.

SAVE ME.

CHAPTER 6

Davia flinched, as if the words had just jumped out and slapped her. She hugged herself, hoping to stop the sudden trembling of her hands. A zillion questions stormed inside her. Who had etched SAVE ME into the glass? How? When? And why? Did Aunt Mari know the answers? Did Emilie? Would either of them tell?

"Hurry up, Davia!" Mom yelled. "It's starting to rain."

Fat drops hammered the roof over the porch. The air smelled suddenly like earth. Davia made a run for it, clattering down the stairs.

She grabbed Mom's arm and pulled her along the path. Already that bloody tissue was soaked and plastered like a cast to her big toe. The scent of damp dirt filled Davia's lungs. Mom's curly gray hair melted flat and stuck to her face. She was laughing, though, and Davia thought she looked beautiful, all wet and scrubbed clean. Dad, with a huge yellow umbrella, was coming toward them like sunshine.

"Some walk," he said. "You should have worn swimsuits."

Davia ducked for cover. Dad reeled Mom in with his free arm. First he kissed her forehead. Then he planted a big smack on her lips. It had been awhile since Davia had seen him do that. Her parents usually weren't all touchy-feely.

"Missed you, Katie," he murmured. "Love you."

Mom's eyes welled, or maybe she just had rain in them. "What brought that on?" she asked softly.

Even though they were all squeezed together under that umbrella, Davia's parents seemed far away from her. No amount of hugging them brought her closer, either.

"Being with Aunt Mari, I guess," he said, and rolled his eyes.

"I take it she wasn't asleep?" Mom asked.

Dad shook his head. "Actually, she was pretty talkative. Got to reminiscing about when you and I were in college. About how we were back then, remember? Do-gooders, she called us. And then she started in about her plastic straw and how her commode needed to be disinfected again. And how I'd better keep that darned cat out of her room. Only she didn't say darned."

Mom smiled knowingly, and Davia tried not to laugh.

"I guess just being with her made me feel so...I don't know...grateful, I guess. Overwhelmed at how lucky I am."

"Lucky?" Mom asked.

Oh, yeah? Davia wanted to chime in. How was Mom's getting cancer "lucky"?

Dad tenderly swept a dripping curl away from Mom's eyes. "Yes, very lucky. That you're still here on this big, beautiful, troubled planet. And that you're well."

"And?" Mom teased.

"And now I wish I hadn't promised I'd help out in New Orleans. I'm going to call my friend and cancel."

"No," Mom said, "please don't. People still need help there."

"You've got that right. It really *is* 'the city that care forgot'—now more than ever."

Mom nodded glumly. "I'm serious, Ken. Go. We'll be fine. You're not that far away. You can easily come back if we need you."

"And don't think we won't call, either," Davia said.

Dad hesitated. "Really? Well, okay. If you're sure." He repositioned the umbrella to give Davia more cover. "So, what have you two been up to?"

"We went exploring," Mom said. "Sort of."

"Yeah, but Aunt Mari's got the place all locked up," Davia added. "We couldn't get inside."

"And we couldn't see anything through the windows, either," Mom said.

"Well, I did. See something, I mean." Davia bit her lip. Should she really tell her parents? She felt their eyes on her. "Not *through* the window, exactly." No way was she going to tell them about the reflection that wasn't hers. "More like on the window. Weird writing. In French."

"Really," Dad said. "What did it say?"

"*Sauvez-moi*. Save me."

"Oh, Davia." Mom laughed. "That sounds like something from one of your books."

"I'm not kidding. That's what it says. Let's go back, if you don't believe me. See for yourself."

"Not in this rain, we're not." Dad caught Davia's arm and pulled her closer, probably so her arm wouldn't get any wetter. Too late. It was already soaked. She wished he'd hug her, reassure her that he didn't think she was crazy. But she guessed he'd used up today's love-budget already on Mom.

Inside the stable, Davia quickly changed into dry clothes, then went in to see Aunt Mari. She'd tell her she wasn't imagining things. Maybe she'd even explain about the writing on the window.

Davia gasped as she entered the room. There lay GG, curled up in the crook of Aunt Mari's skinny arm, her face on Aunt Mari's shoulder. Aunt Mari herself had no clue. Her eyes were closed. Her snoring sounded more like purrs.

Davia hissed for Mom and Dad to come look.

"Oh, no. Not again." Mom wagged her finger at Dad. "*You* can change the sheets this time. Didn't I tell you to close that door?"

"Yes, but..." Dad shrugged. "I thought I did."

Aunt Mari groaned, and moved her head from side to side. Her hand brushed GG's fur, then landed on GG's haunches. Davia held her breath, waiting for a screech. Nothing came.

"This thing with GG is so strange," Mom whispered. "Mari used to love cats, remember, Ken? That little stray she took in? The red tabby?"

Dad nodded.

"Maybe we should try to sneak GG out," Davia said.

"I think maybe you two are making mountains out of molehills," Dad said. "Leave the stupid cat be. She's not hurting anything."

"Maybe you're right," Mom said, finally, and shooed them all away from the door and into the great room. "So, hon, when are you supposed to go to the city? Is everything all set with Juan?"

"He's expecting me tomorrow." Dad turned to Davia. "Last chance, D. Are you sure you don't want to come with me? Professor Vernaza said they have plenty of room. And there's nothing like doing a little community service to make you feel good."

Davia supposed he was right. And some time,

some place, she was sure she would pitch right in. But not there. Not now. Aunt Mari needed her. And maybe, so did Emilie.

"I've been thinking about it, too, sweetie," Mom said. "New Orleans has always meant so much to our family. I'd go myself if I could."

Davia let loose a long, disgusted breath. "Do I have to call Miss Teri to get you both to stop bugging me about leaving Mom?"

Dad held up his hands and backed off.

"Really, Mom, I want to stay. Consider it part of my medical training." And my ghost investigation, she added silently.

"Well, okay, then," her mother said. "If you're sure that's what you want."

"Sorry, D." Dad smiled. "Consider the subject closed."

Davia offered to sit with Aunt Mari and GG while Mom made lunch and Dad got his things together for his stay near campus. Davia brought her book this time, but doubted she'd end up reading. Her thoughts kept coming back to Dad. She knew how important it was to do something hands-on to help after Katrina. Still, she wished Mom hadn't convinced him to leave. If Emilie wasn't as friendly as Aunt Mari thought she was, Davia would feel a lot safer with him here. And what if Aunt Mari died while he was gone?

They'd been told what to do, she reminded

herself. Call hospice first. The volunteer lady had made that very clear.

When Davia tiptoed back into the bedroom, Aunt Mari still seemed to be asleep. But her hand absently stroked GG's fur. Davia snapped her fingers, hoping to startle the cat into leaving before her aunt woke up. But that silly GG only lifted her chin and looked at Davia as if she were the one who shouldn't be here.

Davia sat down beside the bed and waited for whatever would happen when Aunt Mari woke up. She couldn't help stroking Aunt Mari's other hand. The skin felt like sandpaper.

At last the old woman turned her face toward Davia and opened her eyes. "What are you doing? Counting my wrinkles?"

"No." I couldn't count that high, anyway, Davia thought.

"How long have you been sitting there?"

"Not long." She wanted to look at her aunt, not at GG, but felt her eyes dart away.

"Not exactly Sleeping Beauty, am I?" Aunt Mari tried to smile, but winced when her cracked lips stopped her. She didn't seem to realize that she was petting GG as if the cat were a stuffed animal. It bugged Davia that she just lay there. Why couldn't GG act that way with her?

Reaching for the jar that Mom must have put on the nightstand, Davia stroked a thin layer of

Vaseline across Aunt Mari's lips. "You want some on your hands, too?"

Aunt Mari nodded, and let them go limp in Davia's. "That's much better. Thank you."

Davia studied the plastic orange band that hung from Aunt Mari's wrist. "What's DNR mean?" she asked at last.

"Do Not Resuscitate. That means I don't want to be revived or kept alive by artificial means."

"Oh." Davia clapped her mouth shut and looked away.

"Don't be embarrassed, dear. I told you to ask questions, didn't I?"

Though Davia murmured yes, she still wished she hadn't raised the issue of her aunt's impending death.

Aunt Mari frowned. "What's that strange sound?" she asked.

"Rain." The word popped out, even though Davia wasn't sure whether or not it was still raining. It beat telling the truth—that GG was purring. Loudly.

"How very peculiar." Aunt Mari's forehead wrinkles deepened. "That doesn't sound like rain to me."

"I-I saw Emilie," Davia blurted out, desperate to change the subject. "Last night, on the lawn. She talked to me."

Aunt Mari gave a sharp nod, but said nothing.

"She looked sad at first. Then she got real bossy.

She wanted me to go with her to the Big House. Right then. In the middle of the night."

"Oh, my. So soon? You'd only just met. Surely you didn't...?"

Davia shook her head. "I wasn't...I'm not... ready." She glanced at the doorway, bit her lip. Any minute Mom or Dad might walk in.

"Besides, you called out then, Aunt Mari, and I came in, and you were in pain, maybe dreaming, and you said something about *bébés* and fever and—" She broke off, out of breath.

"I was reliving history, my dear, not dreaming." Aunt Mari's eyes flared at Davia like blue flames. "And you must not let your mother persuade you that I was."

"Okay, okay. Just please don't get mad at me."

"I am not angry, Davia. But I must impress upon you the gravity of this situation. The urgency."

Davia's head bobbed as if it were on a spring. Her throat went tight.

"*Belle Forêt* will never be habitable until the last of her ghosts can rest in peace. Only Emilie visits me anymore. I've done all I could to put everything right. But..." She shrugged and looked around as if to say "See how helpless I am now?" Then her eyes went wide, and her whole body tensed.

GG was blinking up at her. A moment later she wiggled onto Aunt Mari's chest and rested her front paws on the old woman's chin.

"She's not going to hurt you," Davia said, in her most soothing voice. "Just lie really still and—"

"Help me," Aunt Mari bleated. "Get it off!"

"Try to relax." Davia was afraid that, if she reached for GG, the cat would rush to get away and scratch Aunt Mari. "Don't make any sudden moves. Just pet her like you did before, when you were sleeping."

"I did no such thing!" Aunt Mari's voice quavered at the very idea. "Did I?"

Davia nodded. Finally, Aunt Mari inched her hand toward GG's back and gave it an awkward pat. She closed her eyes and made a face.

GG kept purring. "See? She likes you, Aunt Mari." Too bad she doesn't like me, Davia thought.

"But the germs!"

"Hey, I have germs, too. So do you. So does everybody. What's the worst that can happen?"

Aunt Mari actually seemed to consider Davia's question. At last she offered up a nervous chuckle. "You make a good point, missy. I'm already on my last legs. Really, what harm can four little dirty ones do me now?" She touched GG's front paw with one finger as if to prove her point. "There. I did it. Are you happy now?"

"You're so brave, Aunt Mari," Davia said. Her eyes got suddenly hot.

"You think so, do you?"

Davia nodded. "Not just about GG. About... everything."

"Sometimes, my dear girl, a person has no choice. One does what one must do. Didn't your mother?"

Davia wished her aunt hadn't reminded her of that. There was one more brave person she'd never live up to. "You knew Mom was sick, then?"

Aunt Mari shook her head. "I only found out afterward. And by that time, I'd taken ill myself."

Davia bit at her hangnail again. "What's it like, Aunt Mari? Dying, I mean."

Aunt Mari raised her used-to-be eyebrows.

"I'm sorry. I shouldn't have—"

"You hush up," Aunt Mari snapped. "Let me talk. A serious question deserves a serious answer." GG stood then, arched her back, and finally settled down against Aunt Mari's side. Aunt Mari brushed invisible germs from the sheets, stole a glance at GG, then folded her hands over her chest. "I guess to be honest, dying is like living, only...smaller. Does that make any sense?"

Davia thought about how her aunt had moved from the Big House to the stable, then from the stable to this room, to this bed, really. "I think so." Mom's world had gotten smaller and smaller, too. Some days it included only the couch and TV. Other days, bed, bath, and nothing beyond. But all that time, all those months, Davia had only thought of her mother as sick. Very sick.

"The point is, Davia, to live big. Do you take my meaning? Can you do that?"

She nodded, but she knew she was lying. Her, Davia? Live big? She didn't know how. Or maybe she was too afraid to. "How...how can you be so, I don't know, okay about everything?"

"Okay?" Aunt Mari grunted. "Is that what I am?"

"Calm, I guess. Matter of fact."

"I wasn't always, that's for sure. The first time my doctor said 'cancer' and 'Mari' in the same sentence, I didn't believe him. Told him I was going for a second opinion. Never went."

"But if you didn't—"

"If I didn't go, I could tell myself I didn't have it. That was my thinking. It sounds crazy, I know. But I hid my head in the sand like an ostrich. Buried myself in my work. Chopped a lot of wood."

"You?" Davia couldn't imagine Aunt Mari with an ax.

"Smashed a lot of canning jars, too. Finally, I went back and took my medicine like a good little girl." She tried to smile. Her eyes glistened. "Too late. And I told God, just let me live long enough to set things right in the Big House and I'll go quietly. For a while there, I think He was listening." She shrugged. "You can't mess around with ovarian cancer. I learned that lesson."

"O-ovarian?" Davia's mouth went dry. "Is that what Mom has? *Had*."

"I believe so. But she was no ostrich, Davia, I assure you. And even if she wanted to be, your father wouldn't have let her. Not if he's still anything like he was in college—a real bulldog." Aunt Mari patted her hand. Davia wondered whether Dad could be a bulldog and an ostrich. Maybe so, but probably not at the same time. "Be a dear now," Aunt Mari said, "and hand me my juice. And get a new straw. Please."

Davia ripped off the wrapper, adjusted the straw's angle precisely, and watched her aunt drink. All the while, her mind spun out a new worry. Was ovarian cancer hereditary? Would she get it someday, too? Maybe by then she'd be as brave as Mom, as brave as Aunt Mari. Maybe by then someone would have found a cure. The little clock on the nightstand seemed to tick louder than ever. "Mom and I went up to the Big House," she said, to blot out the ticking.

"Ha! Katharine couldn't wait to get a good look at her inheritance, could she?"

Davia gaped at her.

"I was just pulling your leg, girl. Not about the inheritance. Who else would I leave this place to?"

Davia shrugged. She wondered what her parents would do with *Belle Forêt*. They'd better not make her live here. She didn't know what the weather was like the rest of the year, but summer was unbearable. And all the time, haunted or not, this place would still be stuck out in the boonies. "Well, anyway," she went on, "Mom and I didn't see anything. You've got all the doors chained up."

"And they're going to stay that way, too. Nobody's moving in until I...until somebody"—here she looked at Davia pointedly—"can make Emilie stop roaming around, scaring people."

Davia swallowed hard. "I thought you said she wasn't scary."

Aunt Mari shrugged. "Well, she *is* a ghost, after all. That's more than enough for most people."

"Shh!" Davia hissed. "Mom and Dad will hear you." She checked the doorway. No one. But she could hear them both talking in the kitchen. Any minute, Aunt Mari's lunch would be here. "Why is this all up to me?"

"Because whatever she wants, I can't seem to give her."

"Why do you think I can?"

"Because you are observant and smart and sensitive."

"And chicken."

Aunt Mari's lips twitched. "And honest."

Davia sighed, and Aunt Mari leaned closer. "I can't know for certain, but perhaps she senses something in you she lacks herself. Some little piece of a puzzle that will at last set her free."

"I saw writing on the window pane," Davia said. "You've seen it too, right?"

"Yes. It's Emilie's."

"How do you know that?"

Aunt Mari gave a small smile. "She told me."

Davia resisted the impulse to roll her eyes. It all sounded so ridiculous. Couldn't this whole thing be a figment of a dying woman's imagination? A hallucination from those drugs she was taking? But then why would Davia have seen Emilie, too? Not just seen, but spoken to her, like a regular person? "Did she say why?" Davia asked, at last. "What did she need to be saved from?"

"I don't know. All she said was that she felt so desperate to leave that room, she resorted to scratching out a message with her diamond ring. She wouldn't elaborate further."

"Well, look at you two. Chatting away like a couple of magpies."

Davia whipped around to see Mom in the doorway with Aunt Mari's lunch. Cream of tomato soup and a grilled cheese sandwich, Davia's favorites. She slumped down in her chair and tried to hide her annoyance at the interruption. Surely Aunt Mari knew more than she'd said.

"Yes, we were," Aunt Mari said. "I've been filling her head with all kinds of stories about our family."

"Well, that sounds interesting." Mom set the tray down and told Davia her lunch and Dad were waiting in the kitchen. "Are they new ones I haven't heard?" Aunt Mari shrugged. "Good," Mom said. "Then you should tell me, too."

Davia hesitated in the doorway, wondering what Aunt Mari would say. But when Mom waved her off, she finally gave up—gave in—and let Mom take her place. She couldn't help staring at her mother's engagement ring with the big sparkly diamond. Maybe like the one Emilie used on the window. Davia pushed that thought away, but her mind reeled back to all those months Mom was in and out of the hospital. She hadn't worn any of her rings back then. How wrong her finger had looked, completely bare like that. Why hadn't Davia noticed when Mom put the diamond one back on?

Was that living big? she wondered. Or just living?

CHAPTER 7

Davia's grilled cheese sandwich tasted like rubber. Her soup needed reheating, but she was too lazy to do it. Dad looked up from his newspaper. She couldn't help noticing it was a couple of days old—one he'd picked up at the motel in Mississippi. That must have frustrated him no end. He liked his news fresh, and with no cable or satellite TV channels, this was as good as it got—at least till he went to New Orleans. Maybe Aunt Mari had a radio somewhere, but he hadn't gone looking for it yet.

"Hungry?"

She shrugged.

"Did Aunt Mari say something to upset you?"

She took a deep breath. Just say it! she told herself.

"She did, didn't she? I swear, sometimes that woman has no filter between her brain and her mouth." Dad shook his head.

"Actually, I kind of like her. She's...funny. And she tells the truth."

"About what?"

"She and Mom both have...had...the same kind of cancer, right? Ovarian?"

"No, your mom's was endometrial cancer. You know what that is, don't you?"

She nodded. She sort of knew. But the last thing she wanted now was for Dad to teach her which female organ was where. Especially since he might whip out his red pencil and start drawing embarrassing diagrams. "But Aunt Mari said—"

"Your mom's cancer *behaved* like ovarian cancer. I think Aunt Mari misunderstood."

Was she supposed to be relieved about that? Cancer was cancer. And some day she'd be a grown-up woman like both of them and maybe she'd get it, too. Still, what was the point of worrying about herself right now? She'd only gotten her first period last year. "Yeah, I guess she must've heard wrong." She wanted to say more, say something, now that they were alone. "So, you're all packed, huh? Ready to go?"

Dad nodded. "I'm as close as my cell phone. Call me any time, for any reason. Promise?"

"I promise." She bit her lip. "Mom really is fine now, right?"

"That's what the doctor says. You were there when we got the good news, remember?"

I'm always there, Davia thought. For the first time, she wondered whether her parents' Total Honesty Policy had been such a good idea. Miss Teri had said that sometimes, when parents are really upset, they don't always pay attention to what's best for everyone else. She looked down, and said nothing.

Dad sighed and pushed his paper aside. "She's a strong woman, your mother. The strongest."

"And brave. Don't forget brave."

"The bravest," Dad said. He scratched the back of his head, and when he looked up again, his smile seemed lopsided. "Hey, don't worry, kiddo. She'll be fine."

With all her heart, she wanted to believe that. But how many miracles could Mom pull off? By Davia's calculations, she'd already had three—two rounds of difficult surgery followed by chemo, plus one other life-threatening complication. And she didn't want to think about that right now.

Dad forced a grin, and shifted his weight in the chair. Davia thought how rare and strange it was that they were here together, without Mom. Surely they could talk about something besides her. But she couldn't think of what. Mom always seemed like the glue that held them together. The longer he sat there looking at her, the more he reminded her of the guy in the commercial who says he asks his kid every day whether she takes drugs. The thing was, you knew he was an actor who probably didn't even know that kid at all.

"Well," he said, finally.

"Yeah." She nodded and tried to choke down a few bites of sandwich. Dad didn't go back to reading his paper, though. He kept looking at her. "What?" she said.

"Tell me the truth. How are you doing with...you know...seeing Aunt Mari like this?"

Davia took a steadying breath. "I'm not saying it's not scary, because it is. But I didn't know Aunt Mari...before." She let her breath out again. "If you ask me, Mom's the one you should really be worried about. It must be so hard for her." Heck, it's hard enough for me and I've never had cancer. Yet.

"Yes, it *is* hard. And not just because she was sick, too. For lots of reasons. Aunt Mari was a special part of our lives a long time ago. Then we graduated, moved back to Wisconsin, lost touch. Your mom feels pretty bad about that."

"Don't you?"

"Well, of course I do. But I'm not the letter-writer she always was."

"You know Aunt Mari's leaving *Belle Forêt* to Mom, don't you?"

Dad looked stunned. "Really? No kidding."

"Aunt Mari joked that was the reason Mom came down here, but—"

"Davia! We had no idea. How could you even think such a thing?"

"I didn't. I said Aunt Mari was teasing."

"Well, she shouldn't have said that. You think Mom would put herself through all this just to inherit a rundown plantation?"

"Of course n—"

"No way. The nerve of that crazy woman!" Dad raked his fingers through his hair. Color rose in his cheeks.

Davia worried that he was going to charge into Aunt Mari's room and give her a piece of his mind. She laid her hand on his arm. "Da-ad," she said. "We're talking about Aunt Mari, remember? She's kind of weird. And she's sick. Forget about it. Don't sweat the small stuff."

He looked at her for a moment, then nodded quickly. "Yeah, you're right."

"Mom can handle this. She's brave. And so is Aunt Mari."

Dad squeezed her shoulder. "Hey, you're no Cowardly Lion yourself, D."

Yeah, that's what you think. Sometimes she thought the things he didn't know about her could fill a book. Like the truth about the day he'd left her alone with Mom. She wished she could get up the nerve to tell him now, to get it off her chest once and for all. She had come so close to finally telling Miss Teri before they left on this trip. But she didn't.

She'd chickened out, as always.

Davia got up to reheat her soup. "Did Mom talk to you about mowing the lawn?" she called from the kitchen.

"Um, no."

When she sat down again, he was making a face like he'd just bit into a lemon. "Sorry, Dad. I offered to do it, but Mom wouldn't let me. She said you'd do it."

"It's not a problem. I can get started as soon as the grass is dry."

"Can't I help?" Davia asked.

"Seriously, you want to mow the lawn?"

"Sure." She flashed him a little smile. "I've just been sitting around...you know, watching stuff. I'd be glad to *do* something for a change."

"Well, why not?" Dad grinned. "Nothing ventured, nothing gained."

***

The temperatures must have really climbed that afternoon, because the lawn was totally dry by early evening. Davia guessed Dad had convinced Mom to let her try mowing, because after dinner, all Mom did was thrust a bottle of mosquito repellent at them.

"Use it, both of you," Mom said, "or you'll be sorry."

Davia remembered the swarms of thirsty blood-suckers she'd seen the night before and didn't argue. "Thanks." She gave her mother a quick hug. "See? I've got my inhaler. And I'll be careful, too. I promise. Tell Aunt Mari I'll see her after we're done, okay?"

She and Dad found two lawn mowers in the garage—a riding one and an old-fashioned push kind with no motor. The decision was easy. Dad showed her how to change gears and put on the gas, then watched her practice for a while. They divided the huge lawn into two parts, his and hers, and played Rock, Paper, Scissors to see who went first. Davia won and Dad said she should come get him from the stable when she was finished, or if she ran into problems. Like what? A tree?

Her section lay on the far side of the big oaks. Flooring the mower, she bounded off. She loved how the wheel felt in her hands, not to mention the power under her foot. Was this what driving a car felt like? Two-and-a-half more years and she would know for sure. She could just see herself getting on a real street and freaking out at all the stuff there was to hit—or be hit by. At least here, she could go at her own speed and take her time.

As she zoomed up and down the lawn, she sang old French-camp songs at the top of her lungs, knowing no one could hear her over the growling motor. She hated to admit it, but she did miss her friends from the foreign language "village" in northern Minnesota. Since she only saw them once a year, they didn't have to know about Mom's illness. Whenever she was with her camp friends, she felt almost like her old self.

She wasn't really looking around, just straight ahead—to the Mississippi's levee in one direction and to the Big House in the other. But when she neared the farthest edge of her section, a bunch of hedges and gray fence posts seemed to jump up from nowhere and cut her off. Lurching to a stop, she killed the mower's engine and climbed down to check it out.

The hedge had some kind of prickers, and it must have been years since anyone had trimmed it. Broken sections of picket fence poked through the branches. She stood on tiptoe, trying to see what was on the other side. Something white. A lot of somethings.

She followed the hedge, swatting at mosquitoes. They seemed to have called in back-ups to buzz in her ears and attack her face, now that the sun was close to setting. If she didn't hurry, Dad wouldn't be able to see to finish mowing. And he'd be gone first thing in the morning.

Finally, on the side closest to the Big House, she discovered a break in the hedge. A rickety gate sagged open. Beyond it lay a strange little graveyard. Strange, because it looked like all the caskets had been covered with slabs of white stone and were lying on top of the ground, not under it.

She froze near the entrance, remembering the last gravestones she'd seen up close. Almost three years ago, now. Fall in Forest Hills Cemetery. It sounded like the title of a bad movie. Why had she begged to go along? Maybe so Mom wouldn't be out of her sight. But why on earth had her parents let her go with them? She supposed this was another one of those "not paying attention times" Miss Teri had talked about.

Davia remembered how the three of them had walked around—a nice little family outing—looking for plots, just like Dr. Tyler, that stupid first cancer surgeon, had told them to. If Davia ever became a doctor, she'd be everything he wasn't. The guy didn't have a clue how to talk to a family.

"Isn't this tree beautiful?" Mom had said. "What about here?" Davia hadn't been sure who she was talking to—Dad or her. And maybe Dad had looked up at the tree, but she couldn't get past the puddle of gold leaves below it on the ground. She kept staring at the new ones, that were falling like tears. They hurt her eyes—all those little dead things— and finally, she'd blinked and glanced away. Why were they doing this? Mom wasn't going to die. They all had to believe that, so it would be true.

"How about over here, Katie?" Dad said. "There's room for both of us. Years from now, when Davia's old and gray and wants to give us a call, she'll remember where we are. By Alexander Bell."

"You're kidding." Mom went over to read the inscription, then shook her head. "That's not Alexander *Graham* Bell," she said.

"Close enough." Dad shrugged. "What do you think, Davia?"

"What do I think?" Her voice rose into a squeal. "I think I don't want to be here, and I don't want to come here again. Ever!" Then she ran, blindly zigzagging between the headstones until she found a path. A road. Anything that would lead her away from the cemetery. She heard Mom calling her, but she couldn't stop. How could they talk about graves and dying? She had never before felt so completely alone.

Now, outside Aunt Mari's little graveyard, Davia's chest tightened. Dumb asthma. As she reached for her inhaler, a cool breeze rushed past her from nowhere. And though the air went sticky-hot again, it wasn't the same. Was Robert buried here? Was she about to meet *his* ghost now?

Davia waited, her heart thrumming along with the mosquitoes in her ears. Soon a heavy scent of gardenias clung to everything. She shivered at the smell. Emilie must be nearby—and this time her parents were not within earshot.

At least she was breathing more easily now. That was something.

"Emilie?" she whispered. "You're here, aren't you?"

As she listened for an answer, her spaghetti-and-meatball dinner bounced around in her stomach. She told herself to just run. So what if she was still out of breath? She'd tell Dad it was his turn to mow the lawn now. What did she have to prove?

As she turned away from the gate, something hard hit her arm. "Ow!" It seemed to have come from somewhere in front of her, outside the graveyard.

Rubbing above her elbow, she looked around, but saw nothing. No one.

Stay or go? Davia stood there, rooted to the spot. All at once, other small objects pelted her neck, her chest, her leg. "Ow! Ow! Ow!" Flinging up her arms to protect her face, she saw little stones bounce off and settle in the grass. Were they Emilie's doing? What was all that talk about being friends?

Davia summoned her anger and took another step toward the stable. More pebbles rained on her from nowhere. "Ooh! Ow! Cut it out!" She winced and rubbed the place on her cheek where one had connected. Clearly, she couldn't go that way.

A weird thought struck her. Maybe she'd be safer in the cemetery—even if that was where Emilie was buried.

The gate groaned as she lifted the broken section and swung it open. "If that's you, Emilie, cut it out!" she said, putting on a brave front. "Tell me what you want from me."

Nothing.

"Fine. Don't talk. Don't show yourself. See if I care."

When no more rocks hit her, Davia took a deep breath and moved toward the nearest—and largest—gravesite. It loomed before her like a small room with no door or windows. Big block letters etched in the creamy white stone said *Lucien LeBlanc 1810–1860.* She wondered if he was the guy who had built *Belle Forêt.* What would that make him? Her five-greats grandfather? Buried beside Lucien had to be his wife: *Hélène LeBlanc 1813–1865.* The dates amazed her. The eighteen-sixties! If she remembered right, Lincoln was president around then.

Another cold rush came over her, along with the feeling that she was being watched. Davia hugged herself and moved along, past Lucien's huge vault. "You're not scaring me, Emilie," she said. Yeah, right.

Then she saw them: a whole row of tiny, kid-sized graves. Four of them.

Davia tried to swallow, but her spit totally dried up as she knelt between the stones. The ground felt damp and soggy. She read the names: *Élizabeth LeBlanc 1843–1844. Félicité LeBlanc 1847. Dorothée LeBlanc 1849–1850. Virginie LeBlanc 1853.* Girls, all of them. *Bébés.* Emilie's infant sisters. Gone almost before they had lived. Davia blinked away sudden tears.

When she finally stood up, she realized there were only two graves she hadn't visited. Bigger ones.

The light was fading fast now. Davia had to squint to make out the name on the next gravestone. *Michel LeBlanc 1831–1853.* Hadn't she just read 1853 on one of the babies' markers? Those poor parents! Two of their children had died in the very same year.

She moved on to the last grave and gasped. *Émilie LeBlanc 1840–1853.* Make that three children! And Emilie had been exactly Davia's age! She sank to the ground again, touching her hand to Emilie's cool stone. "Oh, Emilie," she whispered. "I'm so sorry."

A frosty breath brushed her arms. The scent of gardenia tickled her nose again. In the twilight, she could barely discern Emilie standing before her, that long white dress melding with the white marble.

"So. You have come to see me after all. I told you I always get what I want."

Davia ignored Emilie's last comment. "I-I didn't know," she murmured.

"That I died?"

"No. Of course I knew that. I mean..." What did

she mean? "How old you were, you know, when you died. Or even that there was a graveyard here."

"How old did you think I was?" Emilie pouted.

"Older than me, I guess. How should I know? I never saw a ghost before. And I guess I never realized—" She broke off, shrugging helplessly. "How...why did you die so young?" she asked at last.

Emilie didn't answer.

Davia stood, and took a step toward the ghost-girl. She couldn't believe she wasn't running the other way. "I asked—"

"I heard what you asked. Must I reply? Is that a requirement?"

"I thought you wanted to be...friends." How stupid was that? She just threw rocks at me! Davia glanced over her shoulder. If Dad came looking for her now and overheard any of this, he'd freak.

"Friends. Yes. That is true. But do friends tell everything? All their secrets? You have not told me yours." Without warning, Emilie chucked another stone that hit Davia in the knee.

"Ow! Stop doing that." She rubbed the spot, wondering whether it was going to bruise.

"I can do whatever I want." Emilie raised her chin and smiled haughtily.

"Maybe so. But you can't make me be your friend. And I don't have to tell you anything, if I don't want to."

"Good. Then we are in agreement? Not all must be revealed?"

Davia swallowed hard, not sure what she was agreeing to. Her stomach went tight. Then, from a long way off, she heard Mom calling, "Day-vee-UHHH!" with that worried slide in her voice. Davia had never been so glad to hear it.

"I've got to go, Emilie," she said. "See you later!"

Nice and friendly, like she really planned to see that annoying ghost-girl again.

CHAPTER 8

Dad never got a chance to mow his share of the lawn. It was too dark that night, and early the next morning he had to leave for New Orleans. "You did a great job, D," he told Davia. "Are you sure you don't mind doing my part, too?"

"No problem," she said. But she took care to steer clear of the graveyard. She didn't want to bump into Emilie again and find out first-hand whether the ghost-girl might do something worse than throw rocks. That didn't mean she wasn't thinking about Emilie's family, though. Why wasn't her four-greats grandmother Josephine LeBlanc buried there, too? And where was Robert's grave? She wondered where Aunt Mari wanted to be buried. Maybe her parents knew.

The hospice nurse came at ten to check on Aunt Mari. Davia and Mom waited on the folded-up hide-a-bed in the great room. It definitely felt more comfortable on Davia's butt than it did on her back when she was trying to sleep.

"How long do you think she has left?" Davia whispered.

Mom shrugged. "I don't have any experience with this, honey. Both of your grandparents died"—she hesitated—"unexpectedly."

"Is that worse?"

"I don't know. Maybe."

"Because you don't get to say good-bye?"

Mom nodded. She looked like she was going to say something else, but she didn't.

Davia licked her lips. "The thing I want to know is, what happens after you die? I mean, not to *you*. To anybody."

"Oh, Davia, isn't there something else we can talk about? Like what's happening on 'Days'? I haven't checked to see whether we can even get regular TV reception or what time it's on here—"

"Mo-om!" She sounded like GG's weird Tonkinese meow again. "Please?"

Mom sighed and stared at her nails for the longest time. Davia wondered whether the ridges on them from the chemo still bugged her mother and brought all the memories back. "I don't know how to answer that, sweetie. How can anyone know for sure? People can't exactly die and come back and tell us." She gave Davia a lopsided smile. "That's what religion's for, I guess. To help people come up with answers, whatever they are. Maybe your dad and I made a mistake, not taking you to church or temple or someplace."

Davia didn't reply. Believing in a Loving Higher Power and following the Ten Commandments pretty much summed it up for their family. But she remembered when Mom was sick, how every night at bedtime they'd say the Twenty-third Psalm together—the one about the Valley of the Shadow of Death. Davia didn't totally understand it. Still, she liked hearing their voices melt together as they said the words. For those few minutes, they sounded strong. And brave.

"Mom," she said finally, "I'm asking what *you* think."

"This is so hard for me, Davia. I'd really rather—"

"I know. I'm sorry. It's just that I...Oh, never mind."

Mom rubbed her forehead with both hands, as if Davia's question had given her an instant migraine. Finally, she looked up. "What I think is, a person's body is just a house for her soul, for her spirit—for what makes her *her*, you know?" Davia nodded, and Mom went on. "And when she dies, her spirit leaves her body and lives on forever in a place nobody—no human person—can see."

"So, like the person's still around, always? She's just invisible?" Davia couldn't help thinking of Emilie, and frowned. Hadn't she seen her, heard her, smelled her? What would Emilie say if Davia asked her the same question?

Mom sighed. "Here, try this. Imagine a ship sailing away from you in, say, San Francisco." Davia pictured Fisherman's Wharf and Alcatraz in her mind's eye, and a giant cruise ship passing under the Golden Gate bridge. "You're standing on the pier, waving good-bye. After a while, you can't see that ship anymore, right? But that doesn't mean it's gone. And that doesn't mean there aren't people in Hawaii, cheering when they see the same ship appear on their horizon."

"Oh, Mom, that's so..." Davia couldn't even find the right word. Cool? Beautiful? Comforting? Mom had once told her that the only way she could stay strong and positive when she was sick was to lock up Every Last Thought about Dying in an imaginary little box. Now Davia realized how hard it must have been for her to unlock it. Her eyes burned, her nose itched suddenly, and the only thing she could do with her hands was to grab Mom's. "Thanks, Mom."

Her mother's eyes were watering, too, and she quickly looked away. The refrigerator's hum filled the silence.

"Mommy, that day..." Davia's heart started pounding, just thinking about it. She had to force the words out. "...the day you needed all that blood, did you ever feel, you know, like you were...dying?"

"No, of course not." Mom answered too fast, and still didn't look at her. "Try not to worry, sweetie," she said at last, but her smile looked tight. "We'll never really lose each other. No matter what."

"But if something happened to you—"

"Our relationship would change, that's all. From the physical to the spiritual."

"The spiritual? You mean you'd be a ghost?"

"No! Not a ghost." Mom stood up. When she finally turned toward Davia again, Davia did not like the look in her eyes. "Is that what all this is about? Ghosts? Here I thought we were having a serious discussion."

"We were."

"No. Mari's sucked you into her ghost nonsense, hasn't she?"

"No. This has nothing to do with her." Now Davia was on her feet, trying to calm her mother. "Don't be that way," she said. "If I hadn't come down here to this creepy place, I wouldn't even be thinking about ghosts."

Mom flinched as if Davia had just slapped her. "We wanted to send you to camp, remember?"

"I know. I'm sorry. I didn't mean that."

"No. I think you did. And it's okay. Really." She eased Davia's hair away from her face and tried to smile, but it came off wobbly. "I guess your dad and I didn't realize how much Aunt Mari has changed. To us, she was always like sugar with a dash of vinegar. But she was never way out there in...you know...crazy land. This ghost stuff...it's all new, since she moved to *Belle Forêt*."

Davia looked out the window. Over by the oaks, sunlight was breaking through the canopy of branches, turning the grass she'd mowed there a brighter green.

"Do you think you'd be happier at camp?" Mom asked.

"Happier?" She blinked at Mom dumbly. Aunt Mari would still be dying. Emilie would still need saving. And Mom would be here all alone when Dad was in New Orleans.

"Maybe I should call and see if they still have any openings. We could fly you up to Bemidji. You'd be with all your old friends. What do you think?"

"I think this subject is closed," Davia said. "Dad even said so."

GG raced in then, carrying one of Aunt Mari's straws in her mouth. She dropped it at Davia's feet and looked up as if Davia were supposed to do something. Mom picked it up and flicked it at the wastebasket, but missed. To their amazement, GG chased after it and brought it back again.

"Where do you suppose she learned that?" Mom asked.

Davia shrugged. "Aunt Mari?" She threw the straw and GG fetched it again. Incredible. They were playing together, almost.

Davia saw the hospice nurse hiding out in the hall, as if she didn't want to interrupt. She was making a big deal of putting her stethoscope in her bag, then writing in Aunt Mari's notebook and in her own file. The nurse had bouncy dark curls, twinkly blue eyes, and the kind of dimples cheerleaders have. Davia couldn't believe she was old enough to have graduated from high school, let alone college. She also couldn't believe she was brave enough to see people dying. Every day.

Mom turned. "Oh, Paula. I didn't see you. How's she doing?"

"Well, I think we need to talk about that." In her loose cotton dress and strappy sandals, she didn't even look like a nurse. When she came closer, though, Davia could read the hospice ID card clipped to her pocket. Paula, R.N. No question about it. She was the real thing.

"Why don't we sit down," Mom said. "Can I get you something? Coffee? A soda?"

Paula shook her head. She set Aunt Mari's notebook on the end table and Davia plunked herself down beside it.

"Okay if I stay, Mom?"

"I guess so."

Paula didn't object, either. Davia knew she could read everything for herself soon enough, so the nurse probably wouldn't lie on account of her being there.

"Well, I have to tell you right off, it's a huge relief to Mari, y'all bein' here. Otherwise she'd be in a nursin' home—if we could find her a place—or at our hospice house, but she really wanted to die at home. As you know. And y'all make that possible now."

"I guess I was asking because..." Mom began to cough and kept coughing, like her words were choking her. Davia didn't know what was wrong, but she hurried to get a glass of water. Mom took forever to drink it. Finally, she continued. "What I mean is, are you sure she's not going to pull out of this? Couldn't there still be some kind of a miracle?"

"We always hope for one. Truly we do. But in Mari's case, that seems unlikely. Even she admits she can feel the cancer winnin' now."

"So what's your best..." Mom's voice dried up and floated away.

"How long has she got?" Davia said finally, because she knew Mom couldn't.

Her mother started rubbing that thumbnail again.

"That's hard to say for sure," Paula said. "Could be a month. Could be a week. It just depends."

"How can we tell when...you know...it's... close?" Davia asked.

Mom frowned at her, but Davia couldn't help it. She had to know what to expect. So she wouldn't be as scared. And so she'd know how much time Aunt Mari had left to tell her more about Emilie.

"Yes," Mom murmured at last, "I want to know, too. What signs should we look for?"

"Watch her appetite, for one thing. Cancer makes chemicals that can take it away," Paula said. "Most likely, she'll stop eatin', and it's important for that to be okay. For y'all to give her permission not to eat. And she'll start sleepin' more and more, and be harder to wake up."

"Really?" Davia didn't know what she'd expected. Something more dramatic, like she'd see on *ER,* maybe.

Paula nodded. "They're normal changes as the body slows down. Nothin' to be alarmed about. Same thing for her bein' confused about time and people and where she is."

"She's already got some of that," Mom said. "Confusion, I mean. She keeps talking about ghosts."

Davia wanted to argue, to defend Aunt Mari, but she clamped her mouth shut.

"Well, try not to overreact," Paula said. "Just tell her where she is, who y'all are. The main thing is to be a good listener—what we like to call a 'carin' presence.'" GG came in then and dropped the straw again at Davia's feet. Paula tried to pet her but she darted away. "That's another thing. The cat. Pets are so helpful in keepin' patients oriented."

"Not if the patient hates animals," Mom muttered, and Davia realized nothing she said would make her mother believe Aunt Mari was trying to put up with GG. Not till Mom saw it with her own eyes.

"What else, Paula?" Mom asked.

Davia braced herself for something scarier than sleeping a lot, talking about ghosts, and not eating.

"Y'all may notice her arms and legs gettin' cooler, the underside of her body gettin' darker. That means her circulation is slowin' down. And she'll drink less, too, so it'll be harder for her to cough anythin' up. All that stuff might collect at the back of her throat and make her breathin' noisy. Here. Let me leave you some of these." Paula searched through her tote bag, then handed Mom a fistful of what looked like lollipops, only the candy parts were pink sponges wrapped in plastic.

"What're those for?" Davia asked.

"Keepin' her mouth moist. Just dip it in water and gently swab the inside."

"Is there anything else we should know?" Mom asked.

"Y'all will do fine. And you can call us any time, day or night."

"But what if I miss something?" Mom sounded as nervous as Davia felt.

Paula laid her hand on Mom's. "Don't worry, Mrs. Peters. Everythin' I've talked about is in your hospice packet. Y'all might want to get that out and read it—or reread it—and keep it handy."

Mom nodded, bit her lip. "We'll do that. Thanks."

"I'll be back next week, unless you need me sooner." Paula gathered up her bag and stood.

"But you haven't said how she is right now," Davia said.

"I'm sorry, Paula," Mom said. "My daughter's just—"

"Don't apologize. Please. Truth is, Mari's a little weaker than she was last time. She says the pain is comin' more often. I'm gonna talk to the doctor about adjustin' her meds—maybe get some liquid morphine and Lorazepam, for when things progress and swallowin' pills gets hard. I'll get back to you, and our pharmacy will deliver whatever you need."

"So, she really *is* dying?" Until Davia heard her own question, she hadn't realized that, deep down, she, like Mom, had been holding out hope for a miracle: that Aunt Mari would be like Mom.

"Yes," Paula said. "Yes, she is." She didn't even blink. But her voice curled around them like a hug.

Davia sighed. Mom followed Paula to the door, and Davia could hear them talking in low voices.

Fine. Try to exclude me. She knew exactly where the hospice folder was—on the kitchen counter. It didn't take her long to flip through the pages until she found what she was looking for:

6. Hearing and vision will lessen as the nervous system slows. Keep lights on in the room. NEVER assume s/he cannot hear you. ALWAYS assume s/he can hear. Explain what you are doing, show your feelings. Say the things that have not been said. Encourage others to do the same. Do NOT exclude children. They may want to talk or say good-bye in their own way.

See, Mom? Even hospice says you should have brought me.

7. There may be restlessness, pulling at the bed linens, having visions you can't see. They might even talk to deceased loved ones. This happens as a result of slowed blood circulation and less oxygen to the brain. Stay calm, speak slowly and assuredly. Do not agree with the inaccuracy to reality, but...

Davia couldn't go on once her mind totally grabbed hold of "They might have visions, talk to deceased loved ones."

She slapped the folder closed. Her heart beat fast. "Paula, wait!" But Mom had already closed the front door and was heading for Aunt Mari's room. "Be right back," Davia called over her shoulder, and she hurried outside.

Paula's little black SUV was backed up to the stable. The engine purred and Davia saw her behind the wheel, flipping through CDs. She raced around and banged on Paula's window. She could feel the bass through the glass, and it took a while for Paula to hear her. Finally, the nurse opened the window.

"Hey," she said. "Sorry. Did I forget somethin'?"

Davia shook her head. "I just have to ask you..." Her breath came hard, as if she'd run a whole mile with no cheating. "I read that handout. You know, about the signs of dying."

Paula nodded.

"Is it true when you're dying, you see dead people? That you talk to them?"

"Some do. I've had patients talk to their parents, their grandparents, even. Just as if they were right there in the room."

"Maybe you should know...in case it's important...um, Aunt Mari *does* see dead people." She wondered what it meant that she did, too.

"Thank you for tellin' me, hon. I'll make a note right here in her file."

"Does that mean Aunt Mari's closer, you know, than we thought?" Davia suddenly realized that she needed more time. She was going to miss a lot more about Aunt Mari than her stories about Emilie and *Belle Forêt*.

"It's really hard to say." Paula forced a smile.

"Y'all take good care now. And you call if you want to talk to a social worker or our chaplain, okay?"

"Yeah. Sure." She'd talk to Mom or call Miss Teri before she'd talk to any stranger. Davia waved, and as Paula pulled away she tried to wrap her mind around the fact that Aunt Mari really was dying. Maybe sooner rather than later. They'd only just met, and already Davia had discovered the old woman's soft center beneath the crusty exterior. She liked Aunt Mari's outrageous honesty, too.

Paula's car kicked up so much dust, Davia could barely see her turn onto River Road. Still, she stood there, watching. And coughing. She could barely take a breath before the next cough knocked it out of her. She patted her pockets. No inhaler.

Mom was on her the minute she came inside. "Are you all right? What happened? What did she say to upset you?"

Davia shook her head. She couldn't answer.

"Where's your inhaler?"

Davia pointed to her purse on the bookshelf. Mom dumped everything onto the sofa, grabbed the inhaler, flipped off the cap, and shook it. Davia felt Mom rubbing circles on her back as she sucked two puffs.

Mom's face looked as white as Aunt Mari's sheets. "Maybe I'd better call nine-one-one," she said.

Davia shook her head. They were so far out in

the boonies, an ambulance wouldn't get here till tomorrow. Where was Emilie's gardenia smell when she needed it? Relax, Davia told herself. Just rela-a-a-a-x.

Mom pushed the purse contents aside and eased Davia down on the sofa. She hovered over her, waiting.

Little by little, the cough backed off. The far-off jingle of GG's tags and Aunt Mari's moaning came from the other room. Mom frowned.

"Go on. I'll be fine," Davia said.

"I don't know, sweetie. That was a bad one."

Davia shook her head. "It was the dust. That's all."

"You sure?"

Davia nodded. "See? I'm not even coughing."

Mom made a face. "Not much."

"Really. I feel better."

"Well, stay put. Don't go wandering off. And tie your shoelace before you trip on it."

"Mo-om! Please!" Davia shooed her away, and finally, she went.

Davia sat there, rubbing her chest, trying to get rid of the last bit of tightness. But lately, the only thing that really worked was smelling Emilie's gardenia. Davia wondered if she could still find the ghost-girl in the graveyard. But even if she wanted to look for her—which she didn't—there was no way she could leave. Not now. If she ducked out even for a minute, she wouldn't have to worry about cancer, asthma, or anything else. Mom would kill Davia herself.

She went to the bathroom, closed the door, and splashed water on her face. "What are you, nuts?" she asked herself in the mirror. "Don't go looking for trouble."

But then she thought about Aunt Mari and how desperate she was for Davia's help. How could she turn her back on her, especially now, when time might be getting short? If she didn't find a way for Aunt Mari to rest in peace, maybe *she'd* come back to haunt Davia, too.

Great. A new fear to add to her list.

Davia bent over to retie her shoe. As she did, something shot under the door. GG's straw. Kneeling down, she flicked it back. A moment later, it came again. Amazing! The cat really was playing with her!

Davia didn't know how long she sat there, firing that stupid piece of striped plastic under the door at a cat she couldn't even see. Wouldn't it be crazy if it wasn't GG on the other side, but Emilie? Without seeing, she couldn't really know for sure. And yet she did.

It was the same way she knew that she could keep trying to avoid Emilie, but Emilie would find her whenever she wanted. And what would she do to Davia next time?

CHAPTER 9

Davia!" Mom called from Aunt Mari's room. "Bring me some clean sheets, will you? They're on the dryer."

Great. Another germ attack. Only this time, GG had an alibi—she was playing Straw with Davia. "Coming!"

She returned with the pile of sheets, but the stench from Aunt Mari's room made her hang back in the doorway. It smelled like no one had emptied that port-a-potty in a year. Davia tried not to make a face.

"Thanks." Mom came over to get the sheets, wearing rubber gloves from the never-ending supply in the bathroom. She started to whisper something, but Aunt Mari cut her off.

"No need to pussyfoot around, Katharine. Tell it like it is. The old lady crapped her bed. The shame is mine, not yours."

"Oh, Aunt Mari." Mom's cheeks turned pink. "It was an accident. Please don't worry about it."

"Just put me in those blasted diapers again and be done with it." Aunt Mari sighed. "At least next time you'll know where the mess is."

Mom and Davia looked at each other, then away. "What can I do to help?" Davia asked finally.

"You asking me, sugar?" Oh, please be asking me, Aunt Mari's voice seemed to say.

Davia nodded.

"Put me in that chair and take me for a walk. I want to see the Big House."

"I don't think that's a very good idea, Aunt Mari," Mom said.

"And why not, pray tell?" Aunt Mari fired her one of those blue-flame looks, and Mom glanced from Davia to Aunt Mari and sighed.

"If she wants to go outside, Mom, let her. She's the boss, right?"

"You're darn tootin' right I am."

"You'll bring your inhaler?" Maybe Mom meant it as a question, but that wasn't the way it sounded.

"Yes, Mother." You don't think I care whether I can breathe or not?

Mom sighed again, but said nothing.

As soon as Aunt Mari was cleaned up, she told Davia what pillows to put where in her wheelchair. Mom and Davia managed to transfer her from the bed and prop her up like a rag doll, but it scared Davia how hard the old woman was breathing— and the way the veins in her neck throbbed. Davia couldn't take her eyes off them.

"Okay, double check now, Davia. You're sure you've got your inhaler?"

"*Mo*-ther!"

"Do you two want me to come along? I could leave the bed for later and—"

"Stop your fussing, Katharine. At my age, do you really think I need a chaperone?"

"No," Mom mumbled.

"But thank you, dear." Aunt Mari reached up to pat Mom's arm. "I am truly sorry to leave you with such a mess. I guess the older we get, the more like babies we become, hmmm?"

"It's not a problem, Aunt Mari." Mom managed a thin smile and finally waved them off.

Davia tried her best not to bump the wheelchair out the front door. Still, Aunt Mari winced. "Sorry," Davia said.

"It can't be helped. Keep on going. You're doing fine."

When they were both under the oaks, Aunt Mari tipped her head back and gazed upward at the soaring canopy of interlaced branches. "This is my church," she said. "Robert and I, we planned to be married on this very spot, under these same old trees. We were going to settle down here and take care of my mama and her big sister, Iris. Did I ever tell you that?"

Davia shook her head. "No. But Mom told me what happened—that Robert had...an accident. I'm really sorry."

Aunt Mari bowed her head for a moment. "He was hanging lanterns for the wedding. I'll tell you the truth, Davia. His death knocked the life right out of me. I never wanted to set foot on *Belle Forêt* again as long as I lived."

"So, why did you?"

"Well, your mama and your daddy had something to do with that."

"Really?" Davia asked. "What did they do?"

"They just fell in love, sugar, and I watched like it was happening in a movie. I remembered how it was for Robert and me. Seeing them together brought back all the memories. And I asked myself, 'Mari Henning, how can you not want to be with Robert's spirit? You old fool.'"

"And you quit your job, just like that?"

"Well, my mama—your great-grandma Rose— was ailing by then, and living all alone here. Except for Emilie, of course."

"Yes, of course," Davia said, half-seriously.

Aunt Mari frowned. "Are you mocking me, girl?"

"Why would I do that? I told you already I saw her, didn't I?"

"So you did. But I'll have you know you aren't

the only one who needed convincing about ghosts, young lady. I thought Mama was crackers when I first moved back to take care of her."

"Crackers?"

"Loony. Batty. Loopy. Nuts. Off her rocker. Crazy," Aunt Mari said. "Good for you, for asking."

Davia grinned and gave a quick curtsy.

"Before she died, I promised I'd fix the place up again and piece together our family history. And I've been trying to keep that promise ever since. I thought maybe that would be enough to help Emilie rest in peace but..." Her voice trailed off.

"I saw the little graveyard," Davia said. "It seems like all the LeBlancs are buried there, except Josephine. What happened to her?"

"She married an Ormond, so that's where she is. Out on their place by Bayou Lafourche."

"So, Emilie was her sister, right?"

Aunt Mari nodded. "Josephine was the eldest daughter. It's her blood runs in your veins."

"Emilie told me a little about Michel and the babies," Davia said. "Is that why she looked so sad when I met her?"

"Could be part of it," Aunt Mari said. "Take me over there, by the steps, so you can sit down. I'll tell you what I know, but it could take a while."

When they left the shady oaks, the midday sun came at them like an open oven preheated to bake a cake. "Let me go get you a hat," Davia said.

"Why? Are you worried I might get skin cancer?" Aunt Mari's lips twitched. "A little sun will do me good. Vitamin D, don't you know. I can't remember when I last felt sun on my face."

"Okay, boss." Davia took a seat on one of the steps.

Aunt Mari groaned. Something rattled in her chest.

Davia leaned closer, listening hard. "Are you okay?"

Aunt Mari waved her away like a mosquito. "I don't suppose you know much history about this part of the country."

"Well, I know some stuff about slavery and the Civil War."

"The War Between the States, you mean."

Davia raised her eyebrows.

"Same difference. Down here some still call it 'that unpleasantness.' The thing is, *Belle Forêt* was a sugar plantation."

"So there must have been slaves here."

"Of course. What did you think?" Aunt Mari snapped. "Do you want to hear this story or not?"

Davia nodded.

"Then don't interrupt."

"Sorry." She squirmed, and a sliver of wood pricked her bare thigh.

Aunt Mari folded her hands in her lap and waited while Davia poked around her skin, trying to get the sliver out. Finally, Davia gave up.

"So, as I was about to explain, *Belle Forêt* was built in 1838 by Lucien and his wife, Helene. You said you saw their graves."

"And all the other ones, too. But Robert's not buried there, is he?"

"He's not buried. Period."

Davia's eyes went wide. "What?" Surely Aunt Mari hadn't hidden his skeleton in some closet. Or made him into a mummy.

"He's cremated, dear. Good heavens. What did you think?"

"Oh. Right." Davia let loose a nervous laugh.

"He's in an urn on my dresser. After I die, I want your mama to sprinkle my ashes with his under those oaks, do you hear me?"

"Yes, Aunt Mari." She hoped her face didn't let on that how much this whole conversation was creeping her out.

"You remind her, will you?"

Davia nodded. Aunt Mari closed her eyes then, and Davia saw the muscles in her jaw clench. "Maybe we should go back," she said. "You might need another pill or something."

"What I need is to get in that Big House and figure out how we can help Emilie."

Davia looked from her aunt, sitting withered in the wheelchair, to the steep stairs behind her. "I-I don't think—"

"Are you going to help me or not?"

Davia gaped at her and shook her head.

"You're telling me you'd deny a dying woman's last request?"

Aunt Mari's guilt trip almost worked. But then Davia saw how hard the old woman was trying to keep a straight face, and she grinned. "Don't push it, Aunt Mari. I said I'd help you. But not by taking you up all those stairs."

Aunt Mari nodded, and sank deeper into her pillows. "Good girl. Just see you keep that promise, or believe me, I'll come back to haunt you."

"I bet you will," Davia muttered.

"And I won't be alone."

"Great," Davia said glumly.

"Cheer up. I've done most of the work already. You have no idea how many journals and letters I've read. I should have a degree."

"What did you do with all that stuff, anyway?"

"Everything's in the *garçonnière*. Go read what you like. Maybe you'll find something I missed."

"I doubt it. So, what exactly is Emilie's big problem? She's really kind of a brat, if you ask me."

"I'll tell you what I know, but I need to start at the beginning. Obviously I've overlooked something, or she'd be gone by now."

Aunt Mari closed her eyes and sat silently for a long time. Davia had the feeling she was going away somewhere in her mind. At last, she seemed to wander back to the present. She opened her eyes, and sighed. "I guess everything started going wrong when Emilie was about your age—thirteen, right?"

Davia nodded.

"By then her big sister Josephine was already married off to Hebert Ormond. At least he was young, not much older than she was. And handsome. Not like her first beau. That poor fellow was killed in a duel. Anyway, she was only eighteen, Josephine was, and—"

"Aunt Mari! What about Emilie? At the rate you're not telling this story, *I'll* be dead before you finish it!"

"Keep your britches on, sugar. I'm getting to her. You have to see the whole picture before you try to work the puzzle, isn't that right?"

Davia nodded, but kept her mouth shut about the white circle jigsaw puzzle she and her friends had tried—and failed—to put together one summer at camp.

"Okay. So Josephine was gone. And that summer, the girls' brother, Michel, finally came home from France. His parents had sent him there to sow his wild oats. They hoped he'd settle down after that and get serious about taking over the plantation. But, oh, he was a rascal, that boy. The light of his father's eye. Lucien insisted on the best education, the best clothes, the best everything as far as his precious son was concerned.

"Emilie adored him, of course. Michel was her only brother. She knew nothing of his wild ways—he did all his gambling and drinking and flirting in New Orleans, apparently. But what young man wouldn't find that city exciting? It was the next best thing to being in Europe."

"Is Michel a ghost, too?" Davia asked.

"Well, he was." Aunt Mari's expression softened. "What a scamp—always playing pranks on Mama and me. He'd hide our keys. Open windows. That kind of thing."

"But...but he's gone now, right?"

"I believe so. At least, he hasn't seen fit to show himself in quite some time. Now, are you going to let me finish this story or not?"

Davia made a rolling-camera motion with her hand.

"Where was I? Oh, yes. Lucien's journal. He wrote about the night Michel came home—how the house smelled of candles and roses, how the table was laid with all Michel's favorite foods: breast of wild duck, crab and shrimp gumbo, fried oysters. Lucien had sent two slaves with lanterns to wait at the river. Then a storm blew in. Rain, wind, a terrible hammering on the roof..."

Davia remembered the sound of the rain the day

before, when she'd seen Emilie's writing on the window. She could almost put herself back there in 1853. How romantic all these stories seemed! Maybe it would end up being really cool to stay here at *Belle Forêt*, after all.

"Michel was late," Aunt Mari went on. "Everyone worried that something terrible had happened. But finally he stomped in, soaking wet and looking anything but the gentleman. It was Emilie who noticed how pale he appeared, how tired." Aunt Mari sighed. She herself looked exhausted and, suddenly, too pink.

A knot tightened in Davia's stomach. "Aunt Mari," she said, "maybe this is too much for you. The story. All this sun."

Aunt Mari shook her head fiercely. "*Carpe diem*, my dear. Do you know what that means?" Davia didn't. "Seize the day. I'm so afraid we might never have another chance to talk about this."

Me, too, Davia thought.

"Now what was I saying?"

"Michel came in and—"

"Oh, yes. All his favorite foods, and yet he made excuses for not eating. Said the trip had tired him out, and off he went to sleep in the *garçonnière*."

The *garçonnière*! Davia remembered the strange light and the loud bang from the upstairs. That, and the smell of Emilie's gardenias.

"The next morning, Emilie asked a servant to let her bring Michel's tea and a fresh rose from the garden. He didn't answer her knock, so she went in. And when she touched Michel's arm, he didn't move, didn't turn. His face was drawn up in a most peculiar way. The strange, almost-yellow color to his skin made her run from the room, crying out for her mother."

"Yellow?" Davia asked, wracking her brain for some disease she'd seen on television that had that symptom. Jaundice, was it called?

Aunt Mari nodded. "That summer there was a terrible outbreak of yellow fever in New Orleans. Nobody back then knew it was carried by mosquitoes, of course. Not till much later. And the whole darn city was built on a swamp."

Davia thought of all the mosquitoes at *Belle Forêt*. From now on, she was going to take a bath in mosquito repellent—and make sure Mom and Dad did, too. "So, what happened to Michel?" she asked.

"He got the black vomit. Helene called the doctor, but all he recommended were sponge baths. She begged the slaves to cast voodoo spells. They gathered in the yard outside his window. And everyone prayed. But..." Aunt Mari shrugged, shook her head.

"He died?"

"Yes. And that's when Lucien put all his hopes for Michel on Emilie. He had big plans. His daughter was going to run the plantation—with or without a husband."

"But she was thirteen! That's still a kid."

"Precisely. If only he'd known Emilie better." The way Aunt Mari gazed off, staring at nothing, made the hair on the back of Davia's neck stand straight up and tingle. "The pity is, he didn't. Not really. And neither did Emilie's mother."

"What didn't they know?" Davia asked.

"Just how badly Emilie wanted to pursue her own dreams—none of which included *Belle Forêt*."

"That's kind of sad, when you think about it. Now she's stuck here for all eternity." What would Davia do if she were stuck here on this plantation? But she was, wasn't she? That was something else she and Emilie had in common.

Aunt Mari started coughing—big, wracking, dry coughs.

"We should have brought some water," Davia said. "Maybe there's a hose around here. Or maybe we should go back."

Finally, the coughing died away. Aunt Mari patted Davia's hand. "Let it be, Davia. You sound just like your mother."

"I do not!"

Aunt Mari raised one faint eyebrow. "Your worry warts are showing, sugar."

"And you must have had all yours removed," Davia shot back.

"Well spoken, my dear." Aunt Mari nodded, impressed.

"You're...you're not angry?"

"On the contrary. If I were you, I'd save a little bit of that sass for your sweet mother. She'd do well to hear what you really think, you know."

Davia hung her head, and tried on the idea of actually telling Mom to back off and give her some space. She couldn't imagine how she'd ever get up the nerve. Facing Mom would probably take more guts than facing Emilie.

She leaned forward on the step, her face so close to Aunt Mari's she could feel the old woman's breath. Even its staleness didn't push her away. "Tell me more about Emilie," she said. "Tell me everything you know."

"Where should I start?" Aunt Mari stroked her chin. "It's taken me years to go through her things—her journals, her letters to Michel. He saved them all, you know. Tied them up in a ribbon when he was abroad and brought them home. I must say, I picked up quite a bit of French when I lived in New Orleans, but I was far from a serious student. Translating everything would have been so much easier if years ago I hadn't concentrated on learning Latin. Now there's a dead language for you." Aunt Mari tried to smile, but then sort of drifted off. Maybe the word *dead* had distracted her.

Davia touched her hand. Small red bumps had appeared on it from nowhere. "Aunt Mari, go back to Emilie." What did she need to know to help her?

"She never wanted to marry, you know. And surely not at thirteen."

"Marry? At my age? Are you kidding?"

Aunt Mari shook her head. Her eyes lifted to the Big House, and seemed to see beyond the peeling paint. "That writing you saw on the window up there?"

"*Sauvez-moi?*"

Aunt Mari took forever to reply, and Davia wanted to drag the words from her mouth. Despite the heat, she felt shivery all over.

"Poor, dear Emilie. I believe she wrote them on her wedding day, though I could be wrong. I think she wanted the world to know she was being forced to marry a man old enough to be her father."

"No way!"

"Way," Aunt Mari said.

The word sounded so funny coming from an old lady, Davia couldn't help giggling.

"Lucien thought a stern old husband would tame his willful daughter and keep her from running off up North."

"She told me she wanted to study medicine," Davia said. "Did her parents know that?"

"They did, and thought it was an outlandish thing for a young lady to do."

"Not anymore," Davia said. "Too bad Emilie never even got the chance to try."

A shadow fell on Aunt Mari's face before she could reply. She and Davia both turned.

Mom was blustering toward them like another summer storm.

"Oh, lordy. She's spittin' horned toads," Aunt Mari muttered.

"Tell me how Emilie died," Davia whispered. "Tell me quick!"

But Mom gave Aunt Mari no time. "What are you two doing, sitting out here in the hot sun? Look at you! Like boiled lobsters, both of you."

"We're fine." Davia didn't try too hard to smooth the attitude out of her voice. Just let us talk! she wanted to yell at Mom, but of course, she didn't. Mom was only doing her job—worrying about Davia and Aunt Mari and everyone else she thought she could keep safe. "We were just talking."

"Well, talk inside." Mom took charge of the wheelchair.

Aunt Mari turned her head toward the Big House and raised a limp hand, as if she were saying good-bye. Maybe she was, Davia realized. As she walked back to the stable alongside the wheelchair, she slipped a hand in Aunt Mari's and let the silence between them speak for her.

When they neared the *garçonnière*, Aunt Mari pointed. "There's some real interesting reading in there, sugar," she said. "I think that's a fine place for a girl like you to visit." Aunt Mari squinted up at her, and Davia could read more in the old woman's eyes than she was saying out loud: *If you want answers, go to the garçonnière.*

Davia remembered what had happened the last time she'd gone there. And now she knew that was where Michel had died. Pictures of black vomit and white gardenias swirled together in her mind. Icy fear ran beneath the prickly heat rash that crawled down her arms. What if Aunt Mari was wrong about Michel—and more than one ghost would be waiting for her inside?

CHAPTER 10

While Mom fussed over Aunt Mari's sunburn and eased her into bed, Davia stayed close and lent a hand. Mom was right. Aunt Mari's cheeks and forehead throbbed a painful red against her white pillowcase. Davia kicked herself for not making Aunt Mari wear a hat. What if she blistered? Got an infection? Davia didn't need to be a doctor to know that wouldn't be good. Maybe she and Mom had been wrong to let Aunt Mari be the boss.

"I'm fine, Katharine." Aunt Mari shooed Mom away. "Please. And wipe that frown off your face. You're going to get wrinkles."

Mom touched her forehead, as if she could ward off the lines.

"Davia, have your mother look at that splinter," Aunt Mari said.

"It's nothing. Don't worry about it."

But Mom jumped in to inspect Davia's leg. The next thing she knew, her mother had alcohol and tweezers. Davia winced as her mother poked around, and finally held up the offending sliver of wood. "Go put some jeans on," Mom ordered. "Protect your legs."

"Yes, *Mo*-ther." Mom really could be annoying sometimes, but it wasn't worth a fight.

When Davia returned from changing, Mom and Aunt Mari were talking about knitting. She remembered her mother trying to teach her to do it when she first got sick, using fat, pink needles. With only one kind of stitch, they had made what passed as a scarf, but Davia never thought it looked good enough to wear to school.

"But you used to love to knit, Katharine," Aunt Mari was saying. "Don't be shy. I've got some needles and yarn up in the closet. You're welcome to have them."

"Thanks, but..." Mom's voice trailed off. She looked at her hands, then folded them together.

"She can't," Davia said. "The chemo made her fingers kind of numb."

Aunt Mari clamped her lips shut. After a long moment, she said, "Of course. How thoughtless of me. I'm sorry, dear. You look so well, I guess sometimes I forget."

"Some days I do, too." Mom eased a string of Aunt Mari's hair back off her face.

I don't, Davia thought.

"Would you like anything, Aunt Mari?" Mom rushed on. "Fresh juice? I could turn on some music."

Aunt Mari closed her eyes and winced. "When can I have another pill?" she asked finally.

Mom looked at her watch. "Not for another hour."

"How about if I read to you?" Davia said. "Something boring, guaranteed to put you to sleep."

"Read to me?" Aunt Mari looked out the window, toward the *garçonnière*. Though her voice stayed steady and her expression didn't change, Davia sensed a kind of excitement in her. "No, Davia, I think you need a break from a dying old lady. Why don't you go explore the *garçonnière*? Maybe you'll find something interesting in there." Her strange look made something flutter in Davia's stomach.

"It's getting late. I'll go start supper," Mom said. "Anything in particular you'd like, Aunt Mari?"

"Yes. Tongue."

Davia blinked at her. "What did you say?"

"You heard me. Tongue. Beef tongue. It's quite a delicacy."

Mom stared at Aunt Mari. If she'd been looking at Davia, she'd surely have seen her turning green. There was no way Davia was going to even taste something like that. Finally Mom said, "I don't suppose you have one? I mean, an extra one?"

Davia tried to squelch a giggle. It came out like a hiccup.

"Very funny, Katharine. It sounds like Kenneth's strange humor is rubbing off on you."

"No," Davia said. "Mom's funnier. Definitely."

Aunt Mari grunted. "It just so happens, I do have some tongue. In the freezer. One of my volunteers picked it up for me in town last week." Davia grinned at the image of someone picking up a tongue. "Wasn't that sweet of her?"

"Very." Mom had this I'm-going-to-heave look that she used to get with chemo. "What am I supposed to do with a frozen tongue?"

"Hold it," Aunt Mari snapped.

Mom's mouth dropped open in surprise, but the old woman's eyes were laughing.

"Or maybe let the cat get it," Davia said.

Mom groaned, and waved them both away. "Stop! Enough, you two! I'll cook it already. Just tell me how."

"I am so out of here," Davia said, and headed for the front door. Last she heard, Mom and Aunt Mari were talking about pot roasting that tongue like Grandma Henning used to do. Davia wondered what Dad would be eating tonight in New Orleans. Not that she wished she'd gone with him. She had something very important to do right here.

Ahead of her, the black-capped roof of the *garçonnière* poked through the humid air. Davia forced herself toward it, her chest tightening. She whirled about to see whether only her footprints were following her. Something was. She could feel a pocket of cold air pressing at her back.

She sniffed, hoping for gardenia, but detected only dust and grass and summer. She remembered Emilie's moan that first time Davia had fled the *garçonnière*: No-o-o-o-o. Don't go-o-o-o-o-o-o-o. Such a chicken she'd been, running away. But that was before she knew Emilie needed her help. Now all she wanted to know was why. And how. If Emilie showed up again...Davia tried to imagine what the ghost-girl might do to her next. She blew out a quick breath, hoping to quiet her chattering mind. Whatever, she thought at last. I'll just try to be brave—and listen this time. I promised Aunt Mari.

The tall arched shutters opened wide against the *garçonnière*. The ones upstairs did, too. No weird light shone from within, and there was no eerie fog like last time. Davia could see all the way through the six-sided building.

Sunset was hours away. Maybe Emilie couldn't even show herself until then. Good, Davia thought. Get in, grab some books, and get out.

She chided herself for already trying to avoid facing Emilie. But wasn't it enough that she was willing to enter the *garçonnière* alone? Especially after how scared she'd felt there the last time...

Surprised and relieved to find that the *garçon-nière* wasn't locked up tight like the Big House, she pushed open the door. Its creak seemed to go on and on, echoing through the deserted downstairs. "Okay, Davia," she told herself. "You can do this. You can." She eyed the curving staircase that would lead her up to where Michel had died and Emilie had found him.

She braced herself for another sudden bang. Nothing came. She imagined the scene in *The Wizard of Oz,* when the Cowardly Lion stared up at the tower where the Wicked Witch was holding Dorothy prisoner. If Davia had had a tail, she'd have been holding it as she climbed the stairs.

She opened the first door she saw. It fell inward against the wall with a groan. Davia swallowed hard, then took a tentative step forward.

She had expected a bare room, with dusty floors and cobwebs hanging everywhere. Instead, she found a crazy, down-the-rabbit's-hole world. Had she just fallen straight back into history? The floor gleamed as if it had just been polished. A tall chair with slats for a back and a porcelain bowl under its seat reminded her of Aunt Mari's port-a-potty. A dark-wood bed with a high headboard and foot-board took up most of the far wall. Netting hung from the ceiling, surrounding the bed like an enormous veiled tent.

As she tiptoed in, she saw white covers—a

sheet, a lacy spread—and something on the pillow. A long-stemmed yellow rose, still wet with dew. She could tell by its smell that it was definitely real.

"Emilie?" she whispered.

No answer. Nothing.

Where could the rose have come from? The bushes she'd seen between the stable and the Big House had died long ago. Like Michel. And Emilie. Davia started shaking then, and she hugged herself to keep from flying apart. This was too weird.

Get in and get out, she reminded herself.

Where were those letters and journals? Scanning the room, she spied a desk. Davia ran her fingers over the surface. To her amazement, there wasn't a speck of dust. She rummaged through the drawers and found several modern-day notebooks. Written in ink, they were full of family-tree charts, lots of writing, and footnotes about where information had come from. They had to be Aunt Mari's! She couldn't wait to read them.

Just then, as she pulled out the desk chair, Davia heard a noise. It seemed to be coming from the next room.

She swallowed hard. Grabbing several of the notebooks, she tiptoed out to the landing. She wished she could see behind the other two closed doors. Maybe what was left of Michel lay in one of those rooms, not out in that little graveyard. She imagined coming face to no-face with him.

Although Emilie had loved her brother, he had sounded like a pretty scary guy. A scream built inside Davia. She clapped her hand over her mouth to hold it in.

With a startling thud, the rose-room door slammed shut behind her. Her feet found the stairs, and she clattered down, shivering. For the first time since they'd arrived, she'd have given anything to be outside in the strangling heat. Her chest tightened, and a fit of coughing burned her lungs.

Where was her inhaler? She was sure she'd had it when she and Aunt Mari went to the Big House. Then she remembered: it was in the shorts Mom had made her change out of. She cursed herself for having forgotten it. She needed that inhaler now.

Bang!

She whirled about and stared up at the ceiling. The distinct scent of gardenia rolled down, carpeting the stairs.

Emilie.

All at once, Davia's cough lost its grip, and, for a moment, she stood frozen—and grateful. Then she forced herself to climb back up to the second floor, still hugging Aunt Mari's notebooks to her chest.

She felt Emilie everywhere, but saw nothing. The door to the rose-room creaked open. Davia took a few steps toward it. "Emilie!" she called. "I only want to help you."

Bang! Bang-bang!

She shot into the room. Four books lay on the floor. They seemed to have fallen from a book shelf Davia hadn't noticed before in the far corner, opposite the desk. The air above them quivered like a heat wave over a highway. Davia squinted. Surely Emilie was in here. Why couldn't Davia see her?

"Close the shutters, please."

Davia swallowed hard. Had Emilie read her thoughts?

"Or don't. It is up to you whether you see me again."

Davia leaned out the window to swing the shutters closed. If Mom knew she was doing this—on the orders of a ghost, no less—she'd have a fit. What if Emilie pushed her? The thought almost paralyzed her. No. She still wants something from me, Davia reminded herself. When the shutters moved more easily into place to cover the other window, she wondered whether Emilie had actually decided to help her.

Now only slivers of light streamed in where the weathered wooden shutters failed to meet. Davia could see Emilie crouched over the fallen books. She glowed eerily, appearing to float on a foamy-white sea. She seemed to study one of the books that lay open. At last, she frowned. Its pages turned slowly—and impossibly—then stopped. Davia watched, too shocked to move. Faded, old-fashioned handwriting swam before her eyes. But she couldn't read anything from where she was standing.

"Emilie."

The ghost-girl glanced up at Davia. A strange expression came and went across her pale face before Davia could read it.

Davia's feet unglued themselves and inched her toward the bookshelf. She moved as if in a dream. Matter out of place, Dad would call this. "I-I wanted to thank you," Davia said at last. "You help me breathe easier."

"It is nothing," Emilie said. She bent over the books again, and flipped more pages.

"What are you reading? Can I see?"

"*Non*." Emilie closed the cover with a slap. "These volumes, they are private."

"But Aunt Mari read them. She told me I should, too."

Emilie didn't answer.

"I thought you wanted us to be friends."

"Friends do not betray another friend's trust," Emilie said.

Davia felt heat rise in her cheeks. "What are you talking about? We don't really even know each other."

"*Eh bien*. How shall I help you know me, then?"

Davia shrugged. "I don't know. We should just talk, I guess. Back and forth. And no more throwing stones."

"No. I will not do that again," Emilie said. "That was impolite of me. I just...I wanted you to stay."

"Well, I did. And I'm here now. Doesn't that count for something?"

"Yes, Davia. *Merci*."

"Aunt Mari says you were supposed to run this plantation."

Emilie scowled. "*Oui*. Papa and his plans! He persisted in sending me to mindless balls in New Orleans, presenting me like one of his peacocks to repulsive suitors—whiskered, moneyed old men, all of them. If only my *maman* could have spoken up for me and not sat silent as a cabbage! May God forgive me, Davia, but to this day I curse them both."

"I can imagine. I'd die if my parents made me get married now."

"*Oui*," Emilie murmured. "It was death enough, the thought of never escaping *Belle Forêt*. Too many of us were held here against our wills."

"Do you mean the slaves?" Davia asked. "Or you?" Emilie sure could talk in circles.

"We were all enslaved by the rules, Davia. The ones that my parents lived by till the rest of their days: Speak only in French. Welcome only those who do into your home. Bah! This is America, not the old country. We are all equal here."

Davia nodded. She and Emilie were in agreement about equality and slavery stuff.

"Papa presented me to that toad Monsieur Gustave Parlange, can you imagine?" Emilie went on. "And he promised him my hand without my permission."

"That's awful," Davia said. "Why do you call him a toad?"

"Oh, I am being kind. In truth, he was a sweaty, red-faced braggart the age of my own father. I could not allow it. I would not."

"What did you do?"

"I begged *Maman* to stop the marriage, but she would not speak up against Papa. I even went to confession and asked Father Marmillion to intercede. They both betrayed me with their silence. They forced my decision." She turned her face away.

"What decision?" Davia asked.

"Never mind," Emilie snapped. "It is none of your concern."

"But..." Davia shook her head, confused. Why was Emilie acting this way? "What did I say wrong? Tell me."

Emilie kept her silence.

"I-I'm sorry, Emilie," she said at last. "I didn't mean to make you mad. It must have been so awful for you."

"Yes." Her eyes bored through Davia. "It killed me."

Davia's breath caught. She imagined Emilie not eating, losing weight, dying. Or maybe that dreadful husband had killed her. Or she'd died in childbirth. Tears sprang to Davia's eyes, imagining herself in Emilie's place. "How did you die?" she asked at last.

"Must I tell you everything?" Emilie glanced at the journal that lay between them. "You have confided nothing in return."

"But you haven't asked me anything," Davia protested.

"Very well, then. What is it you like to do?"

"I don't know." Davia shrugged. "Read, go places with my family." Her life definitely seemed less interesting than Emilie's.

"Well. You cannot read these." The ghost-girl glanced down again at the books on the floor, but made no move to retrieve them.

"Why not?"

Emilie glared at her. In that instant, all the books—on the floor and on the shelf—burst into flames. "That is why," she said.

The fierce light burned Davia's eyes. Smoke clogged her lungs. Somewhere, she heard Emilie's hollow laugh. Her first thought was to run. But then this whole place would burn to the ground. Maybe the stable, too—with Mom and Aunt Mari still inside.

Impulsively, Davia grabbed a pillow from the bed. Then she beat and beat at the fire until only the stench of burning paper remained. She fell back onto Michel's bed, relieved and exhausted. I can't believe I actually put out a fire, she thought.

A thorn from the rose pricked her neck. She winced as she struggled up from Michel's bed and freed herself from the hanging netting. Her chest still heaved from her efforts to battle the flames.

In the dim light, she could see Aunt Mari's notebook pages scattered about the room like dead leaves. She sucked in several deep breaths, surprised she wasn't coughing from the smoke, if nothing else. Still, her eyes burned, and rubbing them didn't help. When she opened them again, Emilie was gone.

Flinging open the shutters, Davia let them bang against the wall of the *garçonnière*. For once, she did not even flinch at the sound. This time she'd caused the banging, not Emilie. Light flooded the room.

There was no longer any trace of books. And where their ashes should have been, the polished-wood floor gleamed, seemingly untouched. Davia crossed to the spot near the desk and ran her hand over the smooth planks. How could they feel so cool? She sank to her knees, covering her face with both hands.

All that had ever been written about her family history was gone, literally, up in smoke.

And she was quite sure that the ghost of Emilie LeBlanc was not through with her yet.

CHAPTER 11

D avia raced across the dusty clearing and burst into the stable. She had to tell Aunt Mari what had just happened—and how sorry she was about the books. Guilt gnawed at her stomach as she headed straight for the back bedroom. What had she said to make Emilie so mad? Maybe Aunt Mari would know.

The smell of sautéed onions filled the apartment and tickled her nose. Surely Mom hadn't cooked that tongue already and eaten without her. On second thought, Davia hoped Mom had—she'd gladly fix herself another grilled cheese sandwich.

"Aunt Mari, I—" She broke off at the sight of her sleeping aunt. GG lay alongside the old woman, as if standing guard. But Mom was nowhere around.

Unable to find her in the kitchen, where steam escaped from a chattering pot on the stove top, Davia checked the other bedroom. From the doorway, she saw Mom resting on her bed. Yellow earphones looked like a plastic headband in her gray hair. Her eyes were closed. She looked so calm that Davia wondered what she was listening to—music or a relaxation tape?

She remembered the special recording they'd made to help Mom get ready for her second surgery. Her cancer support group doctor had even come to the house with a script for what they should say on it to help Mom heal faster. With a sturdy black tape recorder planted in the middle of the kitchen table, they'd all sat around, calming themselves for the task at hand. Soothing Chilean pan flute music played in the background. The red light on the recorder blinked as they passed the script round and round among the three of them, reading over and over again the special words—magic words, Davia thought—that they hoped would help her.

A familiar tightness climbed in Davia's chest. Surely her mother was listening to something else, not that healing tape. Her mind started spinning, whirling around and trying to suck her down. What if Mom is sick again? What if she's getting ready for another operation? What if they're not telling me? She wished she could turn all the questions off with a simple Stop button.

She tiptoed into the room. The sweet scent of vanilla hung in the air. The tape player lay on the bed beside Mom. Davia tried to read the hand-lettered label through the little window, but couldn't. Her eyes went hot and her lips trembled.

Someday she'd have to live without Mom. She was going to die, just like Aunt Mari had said.

Don't say that!

But it was true. And she might be gone even before Davia grew up. Nobody beats Stage 4B cancer forever, she'd read on a medical website. Who was she kidding?

Stay in the Now, Davia reminded herself firmly. She eased around to the other side of the bed, climbed up, and curled herself against Mom, her front to Mom's back. With each breath, Mom moved a bit toward her, then away. Toward her, and away. Davia found comfort in the steady rhythm, in her mother's warmth, in Mom's life flowing through her. Finally, she stopped listening to all the questions and let the tears come.

***

The beef tongue would not be ready for hours, thank goodness. It looked as if Aunt Mari would have to eat it tomorrow, because by early evening, she was still sleeping. Davia worried that their little visit to the Big House had been too much for her. And though Mom didn't blame her, Davia could see new concern in her mother's eyes whenever she looked at Aunt Mari. At least it wasn't worry for herself. To Davia's relief, when she checked Mom's tape later, it turned out to be an old mix Dad had made her. Something mushy and slow.

Davia let the memory of the fire in the *garçon-nière* and her most recent encounter with Emilie simmer in her mind. It was so frustrating that she couldn't tell Aunt Mari yet. Though she tried to read her book, she realized she'd reread the same sentence seven times. What was the point? Emilie might not have been right there in the room, but Davia was already steeling herself for what the ghost-girl might do next.

Dad called just after eight to check in. He said that he and his friend had driven around the city. Downtown and the French Quarter seemed to have plenty of tourists, but many of the neighborhoods were still demolished. Gone, he said, like the people who used to live in them. Davia remembered how their city had welcomed a busload of Katrina survivors. A TV station organized a coat drive, because people had arrived totally unprepared for Wisconsin winters. Her school had pitched in to help furnish some donated apartments for them. She wondered how many had actually stayed in Madison. Since the news media had pretty much dropped the story after a few months, it was hard to know.

"So how are you doing, D?" Dad asked.

"Okay. Aunt Mari wanted to see the Big House, so I took her there in the wheelchair."

"Did you get to go inside?"

"Not yet. Mom and I haven't had a chance to ask her where the keys are. She's...she's been sleeping," Davia said. "A lot."

"Let me talk to your mom again, okay?"

Davia handed over the phone. She couldn't hear Dad's side of the conversation, but Mom's was nothing but yes, no, and I don't know.

For the rest of the evening, between checking on Aunt Mari, she and Mom played Open Casino and ate snacks instead of a "real dinner," as Mom called it. They made a plan that the next day, when another hospice volunteer came to sit with Aunt Mari, they'd either return to the Big House, if they could find the keys, or at least take a walk to the river. Davia was relieved Mom didn't suggest visiting the garçonnière. She had no desire to go there again, not after what Emilie had done. Who knew what would set her off?

Later that night, Davia awoke with a start. Her heart pounded loud and steady in the near dark. Rain gurgled down the window, but behind her eyes, a butter yellow sky still shone. She tried to work herself back into her dream—or was it a nightmare? She couldn't be sure. She remembered a bridge, an arched one, but not what it led to or where it had come from. Aunt Mari stood in the middle at the highest point, her nightgown flapping in a gentle breeze. She kept turning around, facing one end of the bridge and then the other. Each time, she'd shield her eyes against the glare, and finally she'd wave.

Someone wearing blinding white waved back and motioned Aunt Mari toward her. But the person on the other end—another woman, Davia realized now, dressed in garlands of marigolds and black-eyed Susans—stood mute, her arms at her sides. Who was she? Why couldn't Davia see her face?

Since she hardly ever dreamed, the fact that she remembered anything seemed somehow important. She closed her eyes, trying to put herself back in the dream. Where was *she* standing? Maybe with Aunt Mari in the middle of the bridge?

And who was the marigold and black-eyed Susan woman?

Two strong smells battled for Davia's attention. Stinky marigold and... She sniffed again. Gardenia.

Emilie!

Davia shivered under her covers and tried to untangle herself from the dream. GG stirred next to her. Davia reached out, and GG let herself be petted. A purr started deep in her chest. Still, Davia felt the cat's muscles tense. "Don't go," she whispered. "Not yet."

***

"She had a rough night," Mom told the hospice volunteer the next morning. This one was a guy, a graduate student who introduced himself as Justin. Davia saw Mom glance down self-consciously at her ratty bathrobe and knew she felt embarrassed that the young man had caught her by surprise. "I guess we both did."

"Don't worry about it. Looks like you could use a break. That's why I'm here."

Mom went to change while Davia stopped in to see Aunt Mari. If only she weren't sleeping again. Davia still hadn't asked her where the keys to the Big House were—or told her about the books and the fire in the *garçonnière*.

She tiptoed closer. Aunt Mari's face seemed puffy *and* red this morning. Tiny white blisters dotted her forehead. Justin took the chair beside the bed, picked up Aunt Mari's notebook, and began reading through all the pages before today's.

Davia sniffed the air to see whether Aunt Mari might need to be changed. If so, she and Mom would have to do that before they went out. What she smelled made the back of her neck prickle. Gardenias! Emilie was here—or had been. How dare she come into this house and hang around Aunt Mari! Davia planted herself beside the bed, suddenly protective.

Mom called her name at last, and when Davia turned toward the door, she drew in a sharp breath. Her mother was wearing bright yellow shorts and a knit top hand-painted with yellow flowers—black-eyed Susans! "You ready to go?"

Davia stalled. She couldn't help remembering the images from her dream. What connection did Mom have in it with Aunt Mari? Why had she stood mute, her arms at her sides? Were both she and Davia powerless to keep Emilie from stealing Aunt Mari away from them?

"Maybe we should wait till she wakes up," Davia said, "so we can get the keys. Anyway, isn't it still raining?"

"No, it's stopped."

"Yeah, but..." Davia remembered Aunt Mari on the dream-bridge. She didn't want to make it easy for Aunt Mari to cross over to Emilie's side. Everything in her wanted to stay. "It's probably muddy out. We'll wreck our shoes."

"Don't be silly. It hardly rained at all."

"Still, we should have gotten the keys," Davia tried. It was as good an excuse for staying with Aunt Mari as she could come up with.

"She was either sleeping or in pain, sweetie," Mom said. "It was hardly the time to ask."

Davia considered whether she might search for them herself, but rejected the idea. She wasn't a sneak, and what if Aunt Mari woke up and caught her? "Couldn't we just wait—"

"Honestly, Davia." Mom clicked her tongue. "If I didn't know better, I'd think you'd rather be with Aunt Mari than with me." She pretended to pout.

"Come on. We have to get out, get some air. Both of us. I just need to" —her pale green eyes drifted from Davia's and stared out the window toward the *garçonnière*— "get away." Davia heard and saw sadness in the same moment.

"Your mom's right," Justin cut in. "Don't worry. I'll take good care of your aunt."

"See?" Mom said. "Come on, honey. She's in good hands."

Yeah, right, Davia thought. All her mother saw was him. What about Emilie?

Mom wrote down her cell number for Justin, and Davia finally followed her out of the room. From the closet, her mother grabbed that big yellow umbrella—just in case. Then they set off. For a long time, neither of them said anything. Davia impulsively laced her fingers through Mom's.

Mom cocked her head and her expression went soft. "I was starting to think you'd gone and grown up on me."

"Not all the way grown up."

"I'm glad."

By the time they reached River Road, Davia realized Mom hadn't asked about her inhaler this time. Good. Her mother was making progress.

"I can't wait to see the Mississippi up close and personal," Mom said.

They had just scrambled up the grassy slope to the top of the levee when Mom stumbled. She fell to her knees in the crushed shells and gravel, and caught herself with both hands. The umbrella went flying.

"Are you okay? Are you bleeding?" Davia bent over to get a better look.

Mom stood gingerly, flicking away a pebble still embedded in one knee. "Honestly, Davia, would you stop hovering? I'm fine."

"Me? Hovering?"

"Yes, you, and it drives me crazy."

"I drive *you* crazy? Ha! That's a good one."

Mom said nothing.

"What's the point of thinking for myself," Davia went on, "when you always do it for me?" She stopped, breathless but strangely triumphant.

Mom turned back for a moment. Her lips parted and Davia expected her to yell at her, but she didn't. Instead, she kept walking toward a break in the willows that rose up to block any view of the river.

Davia hurried after her. "Mommy, don't be like that."

Her mother still hadn't spoken by the time they reached the clearing. The Mississippi wasn't nearly as wide as Davia had expected. Only a few barges made their way down the channel. She couldn't see any houses on the other side because of the levee. The water's glare hurt her eyes, and when she squinched them up, she could feel a headache coming on. Already the day pressed close around her. If only the river hadn't looked brown as cocoa, she would have considered wading in to cool off. No, wait. It was probably full of snakes. Scratch that idea. She imagined making up with Mom and hopping aboard one of those barges. They'd steam down to New Orleans—just like Michel had—and surprise Dad. As long as Aunt Mari had Justin there, she'd be fine, Davia told herself.

"Talk to me, Mom. Say something."

"I think you've said it all, young lady."

"Don't be mad. Can't we just try to...I don't know...give each other some space? Please?" Davia searched her face, but Mom wouldn't look at her. "I will if you will."

Mom did not reply. She breathed deeply and closed her eyes. Maybe she was counting to ten in three languages. Or maybe she was leaving Davia and going to the "Special Place" they talked about on one of her relaxation tapes.

Suddenly, Davia started coughing. Her breath squeaked and whistled in her ears.

Mom eyed her sharply, her forehead wrinkling, as she pressed her lips together. "Am I allowed to do something?" she said at last.

Davia nodded, unable to speak. Mom fished the inhaler from Davia's tight hip pocket and handed it over. Davia sucked medicine from it twice, but nothing happened. She felt Mom rubbing her back.

Coughing, still coughing.

Emilie, help! I need you! her mind cried.

Her mother's face went white as she hustled Davia down the levee and back toward *Belle Forêt*. She fumbled with her cell phone and muttered something under her breath. "No reception!"

They'd walked so far along the river that now the little graveyard stood between them and the stable. Maybe Emilie would be there. Maybe she'd help her, like all those other times. Or was she still mad? Even though Davia kept coughing, she tried to steer Mom toward the cemetery.

"No, this way," Mom said, grabbing her arm. "It's shorter." Again, she tried her cell phone, but snapped it closed in disgust.

Davia shook her head, still gasping for air. "Wait...you'll...see-e-e-e..." She couldn't explain. They had to get to the LeBlanc family burial ground. She had to smell that gardenia again. Had to breathe. She pulled away from her mother.

"Where are you going? Stop! Come back here!" Mom's voice followed Davia into the graveyard.

Davia wove among the white marble tombs, coughing loud enough to wake the dead—or at least Emilie, she hoped. Find me, she begged silently. Find me here. Now. At Emilie's crypt, she fell to her knees, still fighting for breath. Cold and damp raced up and through her, as if she were a candlewick.

Mom's hands fluttered around Davia like frantic

white birds. "Come on! We've got to get out of here and get help."

"Help...coming." Davia closed her eyes. Emilie had rescued her before. Wherever she was, she had to hear the coughing, she had to sense Davia calling her. Mom's hands were on her back now, her breath in Davia's face. It still held a trace of mint.

The grass shivered around Davia. She sucked another breath through her mouth, through her nose. Sweet, sweet gardenia filled her lungs. Finally!

Her cough died as quickly as it had started. Her eyes burned with grateful tears. Kissing her fingers, she touched them to Emilie's tombstone. "Thank you, Emilie," she whispered hoarsely.

Mom knelt beside her, blinking in amazement. "Oh, my God! It's over! Are you all right?"

Davia nodded. Her chest was still heaving, but her breathing slowly returned to normal. How could she explain this to Mom?

"Davia." Mom turned Davia's face toward hers. Her hands felt cold against Davia's burning cheeks. "I'm so relieved."

"I knew I'd be okay." She hesitated, unable to tell her mother about Emilie. She would never understand. "I was here before. The day I mowed the lawn, remember? I got an attack and...this place had a smell that made me better. Like magic, sort of."

Mom sniffed once, twice, then frowned. "Some kind of flower?"

"Gardenia."

"Gardenia? I don't think so, honey. They're still in season, but I haven't seen any flowers at all since we got here and..." Her voice trailed off as she scanned the cemetery and gasped. It seemed she was seeing all the babies' gravesites for the first time. "Oh, my. Look how tiny they are. And how many there are."

Davia only nodded.

"Come on, sweetie. Let's get out of this sad place."

"Mom, wait. Aren't you curious? Don't you wonder about them?"

Mom shook her head, scrambled up from her knees. They were muddy and grass-stained, but her yellow shorts were untouched. "It was their time to go," she said. "I have to believe that." She turned toward the little gate and held out her hand. "Come on, now. This is no place for us. No place at all."

Davia rose slowly. "Thank you, Emilie," she whispered again. "I owe you big time." Then, sucking one last sweet breath of gardenia, she took Mom's hand.

CHAPTER 12

Justin met Davia and her mother at the front door. "Well, she's awake," he said. He made it sound like they'd better watch out.

"What's the matter?" Davia blinked up at him. He'd only just met Aunt Mari. How dare he talk about her in that tone!

"Nothing. She's just in a mood, that's all. I offered her some lunch, but she practically threw the plate at me. Said I hadn't sterilized it properly. That I was supposed to use Lysol."

Davia bit back a giggle. "That's our Aunt Mari."

"I'm sorry, Justin," Mom said. "I'll talk to her. You go on."

"But I'm scheduled till two," he said.

"It's okay. We can handle it. Anything else?"

"Well, she's still looking pretty flushed."

"Sunburn," Davia said. Geez, didn't the guy have eyes?

"I know, but..." Justin's voice seemed to catch. "I

think she's running a fever, too. I was just going to check it out and call Paula."

A fever! Davia knew what that meant. Some kind of infection. She didn't wait to hear more. Zipping into Aunt Mari's bathroom, she wet a washrag and brought it in to her aunt. When she draped it across the old woman's forehead, little droplets fell like tears on the pillow. "Here. See if this helps."

Aunt Mari narrowed her eyes at Davia. She motioned her closer. "Gardenias," she muttered.

Davia nodded. "Emilie saved me again," she whispered.

"Good. Very good. But I think time's running out on us saving *her*."

"Don't say that." Davia sank into the chair beside the bed. It still felt warm.

"Just because you don't like hearing it," Aunt Mari said, "doesn't make it untrue."

Davia bit the inside of her cheek and looked away. The little travel clock said it was barely noon. Its steady tick scolded her for thinking it had to be later. "What do I need to do?" she asked at last.

Aunt Mari licked her dry lips and leaned closer. "Go see Emilie again. At the Big House."

"Okay." Davia gulped. Rocks. Fire. What would Emilie surprise her with next?

"Take the keys." Aunt Mari raised a bony finger and pointed across the room to where the perfume bottles—and Robert's urn—caught the light. "See that little brass box? In there."

Davia nodded, but didn't move. Aunt Mari's eyes burned through her.

"You don't mean now, right? Not while Mom's here."

"Emilie will send for you. Watch for—" Aunt Mari broke off, coughing. Her narrow chest worked for breath, and finally her mouth moved as if she were trying to chew something. Davia grabbed her aunt's juice and touched the straw to her lips, but Aunt Mari shook her head.

"You've got to drink something," Davia said. "You'll get dehydrated."

"So?"

"So...I don't want you to, okay? I need you. Emilie needs you."

"Did you look at those journals?" Aunt Mari said, changing the subject from drinking her juice.

Fine. Don't drink. It's your fever, Davia thought. "Um, the journals..." She debated whether to tell Aunt Mari what had happened in the *garçonnière*. She didn't want to upset her. But maybe her aunt might understand what she had done to set Emilie off.

"I hope you found something useful," Aunt Mari said. "Any luck?"

Davia shook her head. "About the journals..." she tried again.

"Spit it out. Time's a wasting."

"They're gone," Davia said. "Emilie…she destroyed them all."

Aunt Mari sucked in her breath. "Oh, my. Every last one?" Davia nodded. "Why would she do a thing like that?"

"I was hoping you could tell me." Davia sighed, picking at a hangnail. "We were having a nice little talk—at least I thought we were. She told me how she was supposed to marry this awful old man and then she said something about her parents forcing a decision. I asked her how she died…and she got mad." Davia shrugged. "But then she started being nicer and asked what kinds of things I liked to do. When I said 'read,' she told me I couldn't read *those* books. The next thing I knew, she'd set them all on fire."

"Good heavens. Are you all right?"

"I didn't get burned, if that's what you mean," Davia said. "And the *garçonnière* is okay, too."

Aunt Mari cast her a weak smile of gratitude. "Thank goodness on both accounts."

"Yeah, well, what'll she do next?"

Aunt Mari shrugged. "It's a mystery. But I honestly don't think she'll harm you, dear."

"Maybe not, but the thought of seeing her again totally freaks me out. I just know she hates me."

"No, she doesn't. Didn't you say she just saved you from an asthma attack?"

"Yes, but..." Davia pondered that confusing fact. "I'll never understand her, Aunt Mari." She sighed again. "How did she die, anyway? Did she tell you?"

Aunt Mari shook her head. "I never asked. Perhaps she thinks it's a rude question." She looked thoughtful. "Did you find my notebooks? Are they gone, too?"

"I don't know. Last time I saw them, they were scattered all over the floor. Maybe they're still there. Do you want me to get them?"

"Can't hurt. Might help. I did spend a few years filling them up."

Davia tried on the idea of going back to the *garçonnière* to gather the notebook pages. She remembered her plan last time, to get in and get out. It had almost worked, until Emilie interfered. Maybe this time would be easier. At least she knew exactly where they were.

"Okay, I'll go," she said at last. "But you have to promise to eat something. Chicken soup, how about that? Or ice cream. Whatever you want. I know. Tongue! Mom and I have been saving it all for you." Even as she coaxed Aunt Mari to eat, she remembered Paula telling them to let it be okay if Aunt Mari wasn't hungry. Still, she had to try. "Please? For me?"

Aunt Mari shook her head.

Panic mushroomed inside Davia. Aunt Mari was really dying. This fever, it was all her fault. She

shouldn't have taken her outside without a hat.
"How about some Gatorade? They say it's not just
for sports. It keeps your electrolyte balance up, you
know that?"

When Aunt Mari again did not reply, Davia
reached for the Vaseline to smooth some on her
lips. Aunt Mari caught her arm and held it fast. Her
fingers felt as if they were on fire. "Get the keys,"
she whispered, "and the notebooks. Promise?"

"Yes, Aunt Mari."

"And when Emilie calls you..."

"I'll go," Davia finished, and repositioned the
cool washrag on Aunt Mari's forehead before she
left the room.

***

Davia had no trouble returning to the *garçonnière*
and collecting the notebooks. They were right
where she'd left them—on the floor of the rose-
room. To her relief, Emilie wasn't there. When
Davia returned to show Aunt Mari what she'd managed to save, her aunt was asleep again. The distinct aroma of gardenias hovered over her bed.

Emilie.

Davia plunked herself down in the nearest chair.
"You're here, aren't you, Emilie? Why can't you just
leave her alone?" she whispered fiercely.

Emilie did not answer. Davia looked around for

her, but with Aunt Mari's room awash in sunlight, she knew the ghost-girl could not be seen. Afraid of what Emilie might be plotting, Davia refused to leave Aunt Mari's side. The old woman's fever hung on. Tylenol did not help.

"Emilie," Davia said at last, "why won't you heal her, like you do me?"

Again, Emilie did not reply.

For the rest of the afternoon Davia pored over the notebooks, gradually learning to decipher her aunt's cramped handwriting. Her notes were in no particular order, but they included stories about Great-Grandma Rose Ormond's father, Daniel; *his* father, Andre Ormond; and finally four-greats Grandma Josephine LeBlanc Ormond. And, of course, all the LeBlancs buried in the little grave-yard. While the family included no doctors, there seemed to be quite a few lawyers and business-men. Whatever the women did besides have babies and throw fancy parties, no one wrote about it. If Emilie had lived, Davia thought, she really would have made waves.

Mom came in several times, trying to persuade Davia to take a break, but she refused.

Finally, she told her mother, "I'm reading about our family history. I just want to be close to Aunt Mari."

Mom cocked her head and appeared to study Davia. "Is that the only reason?"

"What do you mean?"

"You're not having...trouble with your asthma again, are you?" Mom said, her voice soft. She sounded apologetic for asking the question.

Davia shook her head. "Why are you asking me that?"

"It's weird but...I think I smell that gardenia again. Right here in this room."

"No," Davia said. "I'm fine, Mom."

"Well"—her mother sighed—"hospice suggested I write a draft of Aunt Mari's obituary. I'm working on it out in the kitchen. When she wakes up, maybe she'll be able to help flesh it out."

"Mom! She's not even"—she lowered her voice—"gone yet."

"I know, hon. But Aunt Mari wanted it to be done. You know...before. So she could approve it."

"I suppose you're planning her funeral, too."

Mom shook her head. "No. She's already made arrangements."

"To be cremated, right? And scattered with Robert under the oaks."

Mom blinked at Davia in surprise.

"We do talk, you know." Davia bit her lip. Why was she being so hard on Mom? It wasn't her fault they had to deal with all this stuff. When was Dad coming back, anyway?

For two days, Davia waited for the call from Emilie. Why does she keep playing games like this?

she wondered. Why doesn't she send for me? The whole time, Davia and Mom tiptoed around each other like a couple of porcupines trying not to stick or get stuck. At night, Davia awoke several times to gaze out at the Big House, hoping for some sign that Emilie was ready to settle things once and for all. Nothing appeared, including Emilie. But the scent of gardenia floated beyond Aunt Mari's room, filling the entire living area.

As dread mounted inside Davia, the grandfather clock in the hall sounded more like a ticking bomb. Aunt Mari's fever still hadn't broken, and her hospice nurse had switched her to liquid pain meds. She was still sleeping a lot and not taking enough water to swallow pills on time—if at all. Because of the DNR order and Aunt Mari's wishes, Paula explained, the only treatment was for her comfort. That meant no IVs and no feeding tube.

Now Davia listened to Mom read Dad their grocery list over the phone. He would stop at the store on his way to *Belle Forêt* the next day. "And get some raw oysters," Mom said. "She used to love them. Maybe she can get some down."

Davia gagged just hearing the word raw. But Aunt Mari—when she was awake—sure wasn't eating any of the normal cooked stuff Mom insisted on at least offering her: oatmeal, soup, yummy chicken-and-rice casserole. Aunt Mari would take one look and her face would go from white to green and back again. It became like a contest, with Mom and Davia competing to see who could win points with Aunt Mari. So far they were tied—zero to zero.

Again Davia reminded herself what Paula had said, how they should let it be okay for Aunt Mari not to eat. But that was easier said than done. They just couldn't stop themselves from offering her new things, hoping she'd eat a tiny bite. At least she was drinking a few sips of juice or water.

After Dad's call, Mom went to sit with Aunt Mari. Davia was trying to distract herself in the great room with one of Mom's dumb romances—something besides her own book or Aunt Mari's journals—when GG jumped up on the sofa. She stared at Davia as if she wanted to say something. But the day she and that cat understood each other, Davia would eat raw oysters herself. "What is it, girl?" she said.

GG leaped away and jangled off toward Aunt Mari's room. Davia swallowed hard and followed. Maybe the cat sensed Emilie's presence, too—or something was wrong with Aunt Mari.

Some kind of classical piano CD was playing softly in the room. Mom looked up from Aunt Mari's hospice notebook and touched a finger to her lips. Aunt Mari seemed to be smiling in her sleep. Some of her little blisters had popped. Her forehead glistened as if from sweat.

"I thought she'd like this concerto," Mom whispered. "She used to play, you know. Your dad and I went to one of her recitals. She was quite good."

So was Emilie. "She looks really peaceful, doesn't she?" Davia whispered back.

"I gave her a half-dropper of morphine a while ago. She shouldn't be in any pain." Mom patted the chair alongside her and Davia sat down to watch and wait.

Once Dad got there, Aunt Mari would eat those raw oysters. Davia would be so glad, she wouldn't even make a face. Dad would try to make them laugh, and maybe she and Mom would encourage him for once and not roll their eyes. Aunt Mari's fever would break, and she'd wake up like Dorothy and all her Oz friends did when it snowed on those poppies.

***

After lunch the next day Davia went in to sit with Aunt Mari again. "Hi, Emilie," she said casually, because she knew the ghost-girl was still there, lurking around. Listening. Waiting. "Any time you want me to go to the Big House, let me know. I'm ready."

Silence. As usual.

Davia decided to reread Aunt Mari's hospice notebook, looking for patterns. Was Aunt Mari the same—or worse? Was Emilie affecting Aunt Mari's health, one way or the other?

"Still no sign of your dad yet." Mom's voice came from the doorway.

Davia glanced up. Mom looked exhausted, huge bags under her eyes. Her gray curls hadn't been combed and stuck tight to her head. She could have been sleepwalking in the middle of the day.

"Why don't you go take a nap?" Davia said. "I'll be okay."

"No, I'm fine."

"I'm serious. You look terrible."

"Gee, thanks."

Davia sighed. "What I mean is, you need to take care of yourself, that's all. I-I don't want you to get sick again."

Mom ran her bumpy thumbnail over her bottom lip, and said nothing.

"Please, Mom. If Dad were here, he'd say the same thing and you know it."

"Don't worry, sweetie," her mother said at last. "I'm not planning to get sick again."

Davia looked away, out the window, anywhere but at Mom. Of course she wasn't planning to get sick again. But that didn't mean she couldn't. Or wouldn't. This whole thing was stressful on her. On all of them. It brought back so many bad memories.

Finally, Mom clicked her tongue. "Okay, I'll take

a nap," she said. "But wake me when Dad gets here, okay?"

"I will."

Mom started down the hall. Davia wished Mom had kissed her first, told her again everything would be all right. Davia would believe her. She really would. Because she wanted to. And because Mom never lied. Instead, Davia got up, and followed her right into the bedroom. Then she tucked her in like she was the mom, and kissed her cool cheek.

"Thanks, sweetie," her mother said sleepily.

Davia pulled the shades against the fierce afternoon sun and headed back to Aunt Mari's room. "Aunt Mari," she whispered in her ear, "it's me, Davia. I'm here now." It felt weird, talking to a sleeping person, but she remembered what the hospice packet said—that hearing was the last thing to go. "You're not alone."

If Aunt Mari was listening, she gave no clue. Davia pulled the chair closer, then made a sandwich of Aunt Mari's feverish hand between her own. She wondered whether she should wet more washcloths and drape them on her forehead, her chest, her arms. But what if she infected those popped blisters? What if the air conditioning gave Aunt Mari a chill? Afraid to do the wrong thing, she did nothing. Nothing at all.

Silence. No movement, not even the covers. Davia

squeezed her hands into fists. Aunt Mari was still alive, wasn't she? Davia made herself lean in close, and finally she felt Aunt Mari's breath whisper against her cheek. Relief washed through her. She reminded herself that Paula had been here, had checked Aunt Mari out, had told them they were doing everything they could. Maybe so. But was it enough?

Davia didn't want to let go of her hand. "I'm still here, Aunt Mari," she said. "I'm not going anywhere."

"*She* is, you know."

Davia spun around to see who had spoken. But she couldn't; she could only hear. A shot of cold raced through her as the smell of gardenia grew stronger.

"You can't have her," Davia said.

"Oh, but I will. I am so lonely."

"Is that Aunt Mari's fault? What did she ever do to hurt you?"

Emilie said nothing.

"All she's wanted was for you to rest in peace and stop haunting this place."

"And you think I do not want that as well?"

"I don't know what to think," Davia said. "One minute you're nice. The next, you're setting books on fire. Our whole family's history—up in smoke!"

"I have my reasons. There are things you do not need to know."

"Why not? What's so terrible about them?" Heat rose in Davia's cheeks. It was really starting to tick her off now that she was talking to thin air. If Mom or Dad walked in, what would they say?

Emilie did not reply.

"What's with you, anyway? You say you want to be friends and then you act like this? I'm tired of playing these stupid games with you."

"You would not be my friend if you knew the truth, Davia." Her voice was heavy with sadness.

"How do you know?"

"I do. That is all."

"Try me."

"No. No one forgives those who take—"

"What?" Davia demanded. "Take what? Tell me what you were going to say."

"*Non*. I will not. Make no mistake. Your Aunt Mari, she will come to me soon. *Au revoir*, Davia."

Did that mean Aunt Mari would be stuck with Emilie, and couldn't be with Robert? Davia jumped up and flung her arms out blindly, as if she could beat Emilie back, out of the room, out of her life. "I'll be your friend, okay?" she said. "Stay with *me*, and leave Aunt Mari alone."

"All in good time," Emilie said. Her hollow laugh filled the room.

Davia clapped her hands over her ears, but Emilie's voice continued to echo inside her head.

CHAPTER 13

How are two of my three favorite girls?" Dad's smeary glasses and scruffy dark face appeared in Aunt Mari's doorway. It looked as if he hadn't shaved all week. The beard wouldn't last long, Davia suspected, once Mom got a look at him. He held GG in one arm and a white Styrofoam container in his other hand. "For a minute there, when I first opened the door, I thought I'd landed on another planet. And the only inhabitant spoke Persian."

Aunt Mari was still waking up. She simply blinked at Dad. Davia frowned.

"Persian," he said, holding GG out to Davia. "You know. Purrr-sian."

"Oh, Dad. Give it up, will you?" Davia rolled her eyes. GG squirmed away from her and hopped onto the bed beside Aunt Mari.

The old woman's lips twitched but she said nothing. GG settled down by her side, and Davia could have sworn Aunt Mari inched her hand closer. She bet the minute she and Dad left the room, Aunt Mari would actually pet GG.

"See?" Dad whispered to Davia, gesturing toward the cat. "Mountains out of molehills. Just like I told you."

"I heard a rumor..." Aunt Mari struggled to sit up, but couldn't. She fell back, exhausted, on her pillow, which seemed to get bigger every day. "...that you were bringing me something, Kenneth." She stopped, seeming to struggle for breath. "You think you can get me to eat, do you?" she finished at last.

Dad swooped the container onto the bed table and cracked the lid. A weird smell leaked out. Aunt Mari raised her chin and told him to tip the box so she could see.

"Oysters Rockefeller," Dad said, "straight from Antoine's." He sounded so pleased with himself. "Would you believe they only closed for four months after Katrina?" Green flecks nestled with gray in each half shell. Already Aunt Mari's face was becoming the same color.

"Not *raw* oysters?" Aunt Mari turned up her nose. "If I'd eat anything—big if—they'd be those big ones from Acme's."

"But you love these," Dad said. "Don't you remember...?" His voice trailed off. He closed the box and took it away.

"Loved. Past tense." Aunt Mari sighed. "Of course

I remember. My mind's not gone yet. Just half my insides."

Davia shrank from Aunt Mari's words. It took a minute for Dad to find any of his own.

"I'm sorry," he finally mumbled. "I'll go put these in the kitchen." He turned to Davia. "Can you help bring in the rest of the groceries?"

"Sure. No problem." When she excused herself, she felt GG and Aunt Mari watching her go. The grocery bags weighed a ton. Dad must have hit every aisle in the store, unlike Mom, who pretty much shopped only the outside walls. Would they really be able to eat all this stuff? "So how were things in New Orleans?" she asked, setting the last sack on the counter. "Did you get a lot done?"

Dad nodded. "We made some good progress on a Habitat for Humanity house. The new owners are really excited."

"That's good."

"Juan's trying to talk me into joining the faculty at Tulane. He says Latin American Studies has an opening, but there's no way I'd accept it."

"Why not?" Dad always talked as if he just *loved* Tulane.

"I'm happy where I am. What can I say? After all these years at the UW, I guess I'm a Badger through and through."

Davia was surprised by the wave of relief that washed through her. She guessed that, deep down, she really wasn't all that excited about moving to the South after all, no matter how interesting *Belle Forêt* was.

"Where's your mom, anyway? Is she okay?"

"She's lying down. Just tired, I guess." She hoped.

"And how are you?"

Davia avoided his eyes. He lifted her chin till there was nowhere else she could look but at him. "Me? I'm hanging in there."

"Aunt Mari still seems pretty feisty," he said. "I thought Mom said she was sleeping all the time."

"She comes and goes."

"How long has she been..." His hand searched the air for the right word, but for once, he came up empty.

"A few days, maybe. I don't know. I'm losing track."

"What does the nurse say?"

She shrugged. "No one's saying anything, except 'time will tell'."

"I'll call Juan," Dad said, "and tell him not to expect me back."

"Really?" Davia's voice climbed so fast and high, it gave her away. She'd meant to sound more casual—like she really was doing fine. "Oh, Daddy!" She flung her arms around him and held on as if he were a life buoy and she'd only just realized she'd swum too far from shore. Her nose wrinkled at the stench of smoke from his shirt—not

Dad's, she knew—and searched out something more comforting. Lemony fabric softener. Strong hands patted her back. And all at once, she was sobbing. "Oh, Daddy! I can't tell you how crazy things have been. There's this ghost. Emilie. And she throws rocks and starts fires and hangs around and...and..."

"Whoa, honey. Slow down. You're not making any sense."

"I know." She sucked another ragged breath in an effort to stop crying.

"Let's make a call to Miss Teri," Dad murmured. "This has all been just...too much."

"O-okay," Davia hiccupped. "G-give me a minute." Dad would have to leave a voicemail on Miss Teri's service. That's what always happened after hours or on the weekend. But Davia wanted to leave the message, after she'd pulled herself together. Just hearing Miss Teri's soothing voice on the answering machine would help, she thought. At least for now.

***

Late that night Davia lay awake, thinking about what Emilie had said: No one forgives those who take—Take what? And how could Emilie's death have anything to do with forgiveness?

In her mind, Davia shuffled through a short list

of bad things people might do—things no one would forgive them for. Stealing—that was taking, wasn't it? If Emilie had robbed someone, maybe she'd been shot. But Davia could not imagine a more ridiculous scenario. Why would Emilie do a thing like that? Her family seemed to have plenty of money. And how would stealing something get her out of marrying that old man?

Lying did not involve taking. Cheating did—but who might Emilie have cheated? How would that have made her die?

Killing was taking something—a life. But who would Emilie have killed? Not her father or mother. They died years after Emilie did. Maybe the old man...

Davia pictured Emilie's desperation when she scratched *Sauvez-moi* into the window pane on the very day, Aunt Mari had said, that she was to marry. For the first time, Davia considered that the ghost-girl's white dress could be her wedding gown. Emilie herself claimed her parents forced her decision. But if she had killed her fiancé, she would not have died. She would have gone to jail. What other way could she have escaped her fate?

By killing...herself? Davia turned the unthinkable over in her mind.

No one forgives those who take...their own lives. Was that what Emilie was going to say? Davia felt more certain of it with each passing moment.

She sank from the bed to the floor, letting her discovery filter through her. Was it true? It had to be. Nothing else made sense. "Why, Emilie?" she whispered. But when she thought of everything Emilie had told her, she knew why. How could Emilie have done that to herself? Her poor parents. All those babies and Michel and then her, too? She should have stood up to her dad, made her mom talk to him. But suicide! Davia shook her head. As long as Emilie had been alive, there was hope, right? Maybe things would have gotten better. But no. She took the easy way out. She was nothing but a quitter. And a coward.

Takes one to know one, a tiny voice said. But Davia pushed that thought away.

Emilie was right. There was no way Davia wanted to be her friend now. She pressed her lips together, and it felt like she was breathing fire through her nose. Aunt Mari really was crazy if she thought Davia could help Emilie. She never wanted to see that girl—that ghost—again.

Climbing back into bed, she tossed and turned in the dark. She wondered whether anyone besides Emilie was with Aunt Mari. The hospice nurse kept saying it was important for them all to get some sleep, that it was okay to leave Aunt Mari alone sometimes. "She'll choose her own time to pass," Paula had said. "Some patients even wait for their loved ones to step out of the room." But Davia still hated the thought of leaving Aunt Mari to Emilie. Especially now.

After a while, she dozed off, only to awaken suddenly. She thought she heard someone knocking on the front door. She rocketed out of bed, her heart pounding hard. Who could be here at this hour? Had someone called hospice?

She tiptoed first to the doorway of Aunt Mari's room, holding her breath. GG jangled after her. The nightlights glowed, just as they did every other night. Her aunt's rattly breathing both reassured and alarmed her. Aunt Mari was alive, but that awful breathing... Davia shuddered and reminded herself it was normal. Nothing to be scared of. At last, she let herself breathe again, too.

Back in the great room, she parted the drapes and looked out, but saw no one. Should she wake Dad? She blinked hard, rubbed her eyes. Finally, she checked again, and still saw nothing. I must have dreamed it, she thought.

GG followed her back to bed and pushed herself into the crook of her arm. Davia listened hard in the dark and heard only her own heartbeat. Sleep came as a melty-chocolate feeling. It oozed through her, pulling her down, smooshing her into the mattress. She tried to fight it, tried not to let it take her. She had to listen. Be ready. But her arms felt like long sandbags.

Thump-thump.

This time GG tore from the bed ahead of her. She beat Davia to the front door. Davia staggered along, rubbing sleep from her eyes. GG wove between her ankles, fur quivering, on end. Most of Davia tensed, ready to run get Dad; the rest of her—the curious part—looked through the peephole.

Emilie stood in her wedding dress—it was unmistakable now—on the concrete stoop. She looked up expectantly, like a kid come to play dress-up. Moonlight made her glow clean through. She hadn't come to play, Davia knew. But she'd definitely come for her.

Sliding the chain in place, Davia opened the door a crack. As if that would keep a ghost out. "G-go away," she whispered. "I don't want to see you anymore."

"Have I offended you, Davia?" Emilie seemed surprised.

"Just go away and leave me alone."

"Please. What have I done?"

Oh, right. Now the ghost was playing Miss Innocent. "If you don't know," Davia said, "I'm not going to tell you. Now go!" Davia shut the door on her then and pressed her back to it. Anger rose and crashed inside her like waves. She waited until she thought Emilie had gone, then tiptoed back to the great room and peeked out.

Stubborn ghost. There Emilie stood, outside the window. Tears glistened on her cheeks. How dare she cry! Nothing—no one—had made her die young, except her. Not like Michel and their baby sisters. She could have chosen to live, to run away and become a doctor—but no. Davia thought of how hard Mom had fought to live, how Aunt Mari was still fighting. There was no way she was going to feel sorry for Emilie. Not anymore.

Emilie stared at her—through her—for a long moment and said something Davia couldn't hear.

Finally, Davia cracked the window. "I don't want to talk to you," she said. "I mean it, Emilie. Go away."

"You do not have to speak a word. Only listen."

"Why should I?"

"I wish to play a concerto. For you, Davia."

"Go do what you want. Don't you always?"

"I want us to have no regrets."

"Same here," Davia snapped. "Good-bye." She shut the window, locking Emilie out. Not that that would do any good. Hadn't Emilie already proven she could get inside and hang around Aunt Mari any time she wanted to?

Abruptly, Emilie turned away. Layers of skirts flared for an instant, then settled around her. She seemed to float across the damp lawn. If she had feet, they disappeared into the rising mist.

Good riddance. What do I care? Aunt Mari has no idea what kind of a person—ghost—she asked me to deal with.

Davia tried to sleep, but couldn't. A glass of milk and three pralines later, she went back to the window. The Big House stood dark against the sky, but its windows glowed with a strange yellow light.

Fire! Not again!

She considered alerting her parents, but Davia knew that she had to face Emilie alone. Grabbing her inhaler, she raced for the front door. Her bare feet slapped cold tiles. Then she slipped outside.

The early morning still held yesterday's heat. Only the dew beneath her feet felt delicious and cool. The rest of Davia's body broke out in an instant sweat. Her nightgown flicked against her ankles as she hurried closer to the mansion for a better look.

Emilie wouldn't dare burn the whole place down, would she? Aunt Mari would never forgive Davia for letting that happen. With each step, her chest tightened. She looked back over her shoulder at the stable where everyone lay sleeping—and Aunt Mari lay dying. Should she have stayed inside, too, and just called the fire department? No, she thought. Who knew how much of the Big House might burn down by the time they got here?

She sniffed the air for the smell of something burning. For gardenia. For anything. But she could barely take a breath. She sucked a couple puffs off her inhaler, just in case.

When Davia rounded the bend, the Big House

glowed before her. Creeping onto the porch, she approached one of the windows. Shimmering crystal chandeliers illuminated the whole mansion. So it was candlelight, not fire. Davia released a ragged breath in relief.

Dark furniture stood silhouetted against the gauzy curtains, the ones Davia and Mom had tried so hard to see through. Classical music—the kind Aunt Mari loved—floated from inside. Emilie was, indeed, a fine pianist. Aunt Mari would have enjoyed hearing her play. But if Emilie thought she could trick Davia into attending a concert in the Big House, she could think again.

"I hate you, Emilie!" Davia shook her fist at the house and turned away. At least the pouty ghost-girl hadn't started another fire. Still, she couldn't help being annoyed that Emilie had gotten her to come. It wouldn't happen again.

***

The next day or two—or was it a week?—passed in a fog. Thank goodness Dad was there, insisting that she and Mom eat three meals a day and sleep at night. Otherwise, Davia was sure they would have forgotten. People from hospice paraded in and out, reminding them that they needed to take care of themselves, as well as Aunt Mari. But with the old woman refusing to eat and shrinking away before their eyes, they couldn't make themselves leave her bedside.

Davia wanted to tell her aunt what had happened the other night—that she'd figured out how Emilie had died, that she'd heard her playing the piano in the Big House. Was it too late for Aunt Mari to care—or even to understand?

Time seemed to change, somehow. Either hours disappeared without Davia's noticing, or else they dragged by in slow motion. Even Aunt Mari's bedside clock ran crazy—fast or slow, but never the same.

Then came the nights, and the fear that Emilie would haunt her dreams—if she was lucky enough to sleep at all. It was her only escape. But once a dream took hold, Davia felt powerless to escape it:

She was trapped in a long, dark hall, running toward something she couldn't see. Whatever it was echoed like a grandfather clock, and tick-tocked in time to her footsteps. If she walked, it slowed down. If she stopped, the ticking stopped, too. She couldn't let it, though. It was very important to keep it going. Fast. And so she was running, running. But she was so tired. Her side ached. She was gasping for breath and—

Suddenly, something touched Davia's arm, for real. She turned wildly from side to side in her bed, but saw no one.

"Davia, shhh! It's just me. Are you okay?"

"What?"

"It's Dad. I heard you thrashing around, breathing hard." He turned on the desk lamp. "Bad dream?"

Davia shrugged. She tried to open her eyes, to let some light in. Now her father was sitting on the side of the bed. The ticking had stopped and she knew, suddenly, why he was there. To tell her Aunt Mari had died. "What time is it? Aunt Mari..." Davia had let her down by getting mad at Emilie, by not helping her like she'd promised. And now it was too late. "She's—"

"The same. Still sleeping."

Davia breathed again, deep, grateful breaths. Another chance! Somehow she would come through for Aunt Mari. She didn't want her haunting this place, too—even though Mom and Dad said they didn't want to live here, that they would probably sell the property. But how could they, if *Belle Forêt* was haunted by two ghosts?

The drapes were partly open, and Davia could see pink clouds beyond the Big House. "Did you and Mom stay up all night?"

He nodded. "Her back's hurting a bit. I made her go lie down and get some rest."

"Are you okay, Dad?"

He tilted his head from side to side. His cheeks and chin looked gray and sort of grizzly again. When Davia looked him in the eyes, her own got hot and itchy. "Is Aunt Mari...?" She didn't know how to put into words what she wanted to ask, what she was afraid to see. "How is she?"

"Not good, honey."

"Is she getting cold?"

"I-I don't know. I didn't check."

Davia frowned. Was Dad afraid to touch Aunt Mari? "Let me go sit with her," she said, pushing back her covers.

"That's okay. I can go back in."

"No. Really, Dad. You go to bed and take care of Mom. I'll be fine."

He turned away, scrubbed his face with both hands. Finally, he sighed and said, "I don't think that's such a good idea."

Something exploded inside her like early fireworks. "Then what did you wake me up for, huh? Why didn't you just let the little kid sleep?"

"Davia, please. I thought you were having a nightmare."

"It's okay for me to sit there day in, day out, getting to know her, right? But it's not okay for me to be there to...to..." The words caught. She couldn't get them out.

"Say good-bye?" He raised one eyebrow. Though Dad and Aunt Mari weren't even related, his eyes were the same washed-out blue color as hers, and shiny. Davia wondered whether she'd ever see Aunt Mari's eyes open again. If only she'd known yesterday that Aunt Mari might be looking at her for the last time, she'd have stopped and paid more attention.

"We never really know what our last words will be, do we?" Dad said. "That's why everything we say should be loving and kind."

Davia thought about that, and wondered whether she'd missed Aunt Mari's last words, too. Or would she wake up and say something else today?

"You're right, Dad," she said finally. "I just want to be with her and talk to her some more. Is that okay? Even if she can't talk back, they say she can still hear me."

"I guess there's no protecting you, is there?"

"You didn't try to protect me when Mom was sick," Davia said. "Why start now?"

Her dad seemed startled, as if Davia had slapped him. "That was different, D. Your mom wasn't really...dying."

"Maybe we're all dying," Davia said softly. "Living and dying, both at the same time."

"Who put that idea into your head?"

"Aunt Mari."

Dad blew out a long breath. "Okay, I'm going back to bed. Or, if you're hungry, I could make us some eggs."

Davia shook her head. "You go ahead," she said, throwing on her robe, "and I'll go sit with Aunt Mari."

Someone had taken out Aunt Mari's dentures. Now her whole face resembled a shrunken-apple doll's. Sucked in. Collapsed. An upside-down smile above a chin that seemed almost nose-like. She looked like the melting Wicked Witch of the West, except that Aunt Mari was good.

A strange gurgling sound came from deep in the old woman's throat. Dad had opened the shades partway, enough for Davia to see that Aunt Mari's eyes were closed, but moving around like crazy under those thin eyelids of hers. If her aunt was dreaming, it must have been a whopper. Davia couldn't see her arms—they were under the sheets—but every once in a while, the one closest to her would make the covers jump. She sat down, leaned closer, and fished around for Aunt Mari's hand. It felt cool and limp in hers.

"Aunt Mari, it's me. Davia."

Aunt Mari turned her head toward the voice. One eye opened halfway and wandered around, as if it were searching for Davia. But when Davia bent forward and put her face right above her aunt's, that eye stared like it was made of glass. According to Dad, Aunt Mari was only sleeping. But Davia had never seen a sleeping person look like that. Even so, she had to believe that Aunt Mari could still hear.

"You're not alone," Davia said. She wondered if Aunt Mari could see Robert's spirit waiting for her. She hoped so.

The old woman's mouth looked so dry. Davia's hand shook as she reached for one of those pink lollipop sponges. She peeled off the crackling plastic wrapper, dipped the thing in water, and then swabbed the inside of Aunt Mari's mouth.

Aunt Mari moved her lips gratefully, and her forehead relaxed. Her tongue flicked, as if it were seeking out more moisture. Davia obliged.

Such a little thing I can do for her now.

She tried not to think about the big thing—going to the Big House and having it out with Emilie. She felt badly for going back on her promise. How much more time did she have to set things right before Aunt Mari died? In her mind, Davia spun out what Aunt Mari had wanted her to do. She pictured herself face-to-face with Emilie in the Big House and saying...what? What was she supposed to do that would make Emilie go away, wherever it was that peaceful ghosts went? What a pain Emilie was! She had done something terrible that hurt herself and everyone who loved her. But what did she expect Davia to do about that?

What if she *could* get rid of Emilie? She'd race right back here to tell Aunt Mari. She'd hear and open her eyes and come back to them. Davia told herself that was exactly how it would be, if only she could make herself leave Aunt Mari's side.

But she couldn't. Or wouldn't.

"Davia," Mom said when she came into the

room later that morning, "I insist you take a break. You've been sitting there almost non-stop. Enough, now."

"I know. But I...I just can't leave."

When Paula came to check on Aunt Mari, she shrugged and shook her head. "It's like she's waitin' for somethin'," she told Davia and her parents. "Like somethin' is holdin' her back. Sometimes we see that—patients needin' permission to go."

It's my fault, Davia thought. Aunt Mari's waiting for me to take care of things with Emilie.

She tried to swallow a glob of spit that had pooled beneath her tongue. Then, afraid her parents might read the guilt in her eyes, she looked away, at the floor, anywhere but at them.

CHAPTER 14

All the next day, Davia fought with herself about whether to go to the Big House and face Emilie. But she couldn't get over what Emilie had done, how *now* she felt bad about taking her own life. She should have thought about that a hundred-and-fifty years ago. Her parents had probably spent the rest of their lives crying, just because Emilie was too chicken to stand up to them. Stand up for herself.

And still, Aunt Mari hung on. Davia felt more certain with each passing hour that her aunt was too stubborn to let go of life until Davia had at least tried to keep her promise. How could she make the poor woman suffer more?

Now a lamp burned dimly beside Aunt Mari's bed, making her stringy hair look silver, not gray. It was weird how it changed colors, the same way GG's fur did. As Aunt Mari's rattly breathing and the ticking clock marked time, the cat lay glued to her side. Every once in a while, Aunt Mari seemed to hold her breath. Whenever she did, Davia held hers, too.

Dad sat across from Mom, and Davia sat beside her facing the window—the farthest from Aunt Mari—while they "kept a vigil," as Dad called it. They had eaten dinner hours before, tiptoeing out one by one to scrounge leftovers from the fridge while the other two stayed put.

As soon as it got dark, Emilie appeared outside Aunt Mari's window, filmy white beyond the glass. Davia glanced quickly at Mom, but she didn't seem to notice. Why was Emilie here? Was Aunt Mari about to die? Go away, Emilie! Leave us alone! Davia glared hard, then got up and pulled the shade down, all in one motion. Dad frowned at Mom, but she just shrugged. Davia bit at another hangnail and started bouncing her knees.

"Sweetie," Mom said, "I think you've been sitting here too long. Go work off some of that nervous energy. Do some crunches or leg lifts. Or go lie down and listen to my relaxation tape."

"Seriously, D," Dad said. "Go!"

Davia fumed. She left the room without even saying good-night. It was Emilie's fault her parents were pushing her out. If Aunt Mari died while she was gone... She just couldn't think about that. Davia closed her eyes, squeezing back tears. She had to have it out with Emilie once and for all. And

the way she felt right now, she had all the anger
she needed, stored up and ready to fly.

* * *

Davia had no clue what time it was when she
sneaked out of the stable. Mom and Dad were still
with Aunt Mari, and GG lay curled up near the old
woman's feet. Clouds hid the moon, and thick,
warm air pressed close. Sweat glued Davia's hair to
the back of her neck, but she didn't walk to the Big
House. She ran, before she lost her nerve. By the
time she'd climbed to the wide gallery where she
and Mom had peeked in the Big House windows
that day, she was out of breath.

She pried Aunt Mari's keys from her pocket.
With trembling fingers, she opened the padlocks on
the front door. The thick chains fell to the wooden
porch in a deafening series of clunks. Would her
parents hear it inside her aunt's room?

As she turned the knob, her heart thrummed in
her ears along with the swarming mosquitoes. At
least all the repellent she'd slathered on kept them
from biting. Her chest tightened. Davia drew a couple of puffs off her inhaler and stood still as stone,
but the cough, and the squeak and whistle of her
breath, took over.

Then the towering double doors groaned open,
and thick, gardenia-scented air—Emilie's welcome—

tumbled out. To Davia's relief, she could breathe easily again.

"Thank you, Emilie," she whispered, then chided herself for feeling grateful. She had to hold on to her anger at that willful ghost; she needed it to make her brave.

The old war started up inside her. Push-pull. Stay-go.

"Emilie?" she called, stepping quickly across the sill before she could change her mind. "Where are you? I want to talk to you." As she moved from darkness into a parlor that glowed with candlelight, her words bounced back to her from the far side of the room.

She gaped at her surroundings. A baby grand piano with a green velvet stool-cushion took up one corner. Old paintings of stern-faced women hung over the fireplace, above a strange-looking sofa with carved legs. A hardwood floor showed off fancy rugs in reds and dark blues. Lacy white curtains hid the room's four tall windows. Rich gold tapestries fell on either side.

Davia tiptoed across to the piano, half-expecting it to play itself. But it didn't. Even in the dim light, the wood and the ivory keys gleamed. She swept her finger over the music rack. She couldn't believe it. Not a trace of dust.

A shiver crawled down her neck. This place was

like the *garçonnière*—a museum, just like Aunt Mari always said!

Davia remembered something else then, and hurried to the windows on the side of the house. She pulled back the lacy curtains. The window to the right of the fireplace came up empty. She checked the one to the left. Sure enough, there were Emilie's desperate words etched into the pane: *Sauvez-moi.* Save me.

Davia imagined Emilie on her wedding day, waiting in this room in her white dress. Waiting for her father to escort her down the stairs and into the garden. Waiting for the life she had dreamed of for herself to end.

Quit it, Davia told herself. Stop feeling sorry for Emilie. There was no excuse for what that girl had done.

She turned away from the window. "Emilie?" she called again.

No answer.

Stepping into another parlor, Davia saw that this one was even fancier. A huge crystal chandelier glowed like an upside-down wedding cake with a bazillion lit candles. Red velvet chairs with curlicue legs circled a huge rug that looked as if it belonged in some palace.

Maybe she needed to speak French in this grand house. "Emilie? *Où êtes vous?* Where are you?"

A strange moaning filled the air. It wasn't the house. Or the wind. It had to be Emilie. Davia raced into the hallway and up the wide staircase, her sandals slapping the polished wood. The whole second story shimmered with candlelight.

"Emilie, get out here," she said in French. "I told you before. I don't want to play games with you."

The moaning stopped abruptly. Davia held her breath. Moments later, she heard sobbing from one of the rooms to her left. She blinked, letting her eyes adjust to the dim light from a single candle on the dresser. A tall canopy bed rose along the far wall. A set of three wooden steps led up to it. A miniature grandfather clock stood silent; it reached no higher than the headboard. Nearby, a spindled cradle hung between two supports, a cloud of white netting above it.

There Emilie sat in a chair, glowing and rocking. Tears glistened on her cheeks. Her wedding dress churned into a froth around her. In her arms, she held a swaddled infant.

"*Elle est morte*? Is she dead?" Emilie's voice sounded hollow, like an echo through time. Davia had no trouble understanding her French, though.

Who was Emilie talking about—the baby or Aunt Mari? Davia's knees went weak at the thought that Aunt Mari might not have waited for her. She hesitated, stepped closer. Emilie clutched the child as if she were afraid Davia might take it away. But the baby was like Emilie. Nothing but air.

"This is my sister, Virginie. It is my shame she never lived. My mother would not have lost her also had I not...left." Emilie broke off. Her eyes seemed bottomless, without color, as she offered up the *bébé*. Of course Virginie was dead. She was a ghost, just like Emilie. Surely Emilie knew that. Or did she mean...? "Are you asking if Mari's dead? Is that what you want to know?"

Emilie nodded.

"Well, she's not. No thanks to you." Davia realized she'd switched to English, but she didn't care.

"Français, s'il vous plait."

"No. I'm sick of doing what you say."

Emilie hung her head. At last she rose and laid Virginie in her crib. The rocking chair ticked back and forth, then finally stopped. Emilie stared at the candle for the longest time.

"I know," Davia said. "I know everything. So you can stop pretending."

"What is it you think you know?"

"How you died."

"Non. It is not possible you could learn this." Emilie turned her face away, avoided Davia's eyes.

"Oh, yeah? I know you killed yourself."

Emilie seemed to flicker, then fade, before Davia's eyes.

"So it's true. Come back here," Davia demanded. "I mean it, Emilie."

After a moment, Emilie let herself be seen. But she looked embarrassed, contrite.

Davia felt herself soften toward the ghost-girl. "How...how did you do it?" she asked at last.

"I used a drapery cord, in the women's parlor," Emilie said evenly.

"Oh, Emilie." Davia cringed at the image that played in her mind.

"*Oui*. To this day, it shames me that I could find no other way to escape *Belle Forêt*. It was hardly an escape, *non*? Here I am still, all these long years later."

Davia said nothing.

"What I did, it was a mortal sin, this I know, and I may spend all eternity on this plantation trying to make amends," Emilie said.

"Amends?" Davia's voice rose. "You mean, for throwing your life away? And breaking your parents' hearts?"

"It is difficult." Emilie's gaze still did not meet Davia's. "Even now I try to keep the Big House—and the *garçonnière*—as they would have wanted."

Emilie finally looked up and moved toward Davia. She held her face just inches away. Davia swallowed hard and took one step back, then another. Now Emilie had her up against the wall. "Did you never do something you were ashamed of, Davia? Are you so perfect? So above feeling shame?"

Davia squirmed. Her chest tightened. She tried to relax, to take a deep breath. But the air and Emilie pressed close. She sucked another puff from her inhaler, but it seemed to have no effect. What if Emilie wouldn't help her this time?

"What is wrong? Have I asked a question you do not wish to answer?"

Any reply stuck in Davia's throat. Again. She had wanted to tell Miss Teri her secret, but she couldn't. Miss Teri said when the time was right, Davia would be able to share it with someone.

"It's a secret," Davia finally whispered to Emilie. "I don't have to tell."

But the full memory began to unreel behind her eyes in slow motion.

She was there again, in Mom's bedroom, two years ago. She and her parents were watching the Hurricane Katrina survivors crying for help in the streets of New Orleans on CNN. But mostly, she was watching her mother sleep.

"I have to run to the pharmacy and get something to help Mom stop vomiting," Dad had said. "It'll only take a few minutes. Can you stay here with her, Davia? Will you be all right?"

Davia looked at Mom, curled in bed on her side. The covers moved only a little. Up. Down. And finally, up again. Then down.

"Here's my cell phone number, in case you forget." Dad handed her a slip of paper. "If anything happens, call me. Or call nine-one-one. Can you do that, Davia?"

Of course she could. What could happen? She looked at Dad, and saw how much he needed her. He was counting on her to be his big girl. For just a few minutes.

I'm eleven, Davia told herself. Not a baby. I can do this.

She nodded.

Dad muted the TV so only the pictures flickered. And then he left. Davia pulled Mom's port-a-potty up next to the bed, put the lid down, and sat. She watched as Mom finally rolled over and opened her eyes. She had a funny little doll-smile on her face. Like Barbie's.

"Mommy, are you okay?"

"Just tired, sweetie. But I need to go to the bathroom."

Davia got off the chair, opened the lid, and helped her sit up on the edge of the bed. But Mom fell back like Davia's old Raggedy Ann would. "Are you sure you're okay?" Davia asked. "Should I call Dad?"

"No, I'm fine. Just..." Mom made another weird face. "Oh, no. Hurry! Bring me a towel, will you?"

Davia raced to the bathroom, brought her a towel. Mom hugged it like a baby blanket and pulled the covers up to her chin. White sheets. White Mom. They blended together. Davia tried to be brave. Mom and Dad were depending on her. She unfolded Dad's piece of paper and showed it to her mother. "Should I call, Mommy? Tell me what to do."

"Just...let me sleep, Davia. I promise you, I'll be fine."

Davia sat by the bed, and felt herself getting littler and littler. She was not brave. She was a mouse. She needed a hidey-hole. She wanted to run. The paper—the number—was in her hand. But she couldn't move. She had to watch Mom.

Call!

She told me not to.

Call!

Davia had to listen to her, had to be a good girl. Mom would be mad if Davia disobeyed. She said she was fine. She promised. Daddy would be home soon. Soon.

Now Davia wrenched herself free of the memory. Her eyes felt hot. She was still struggling for air, and finally, she started coughing. "Emilie," she gasped. "Help."

"Did my question upset you?" But there was no sympathy, no warmth in the ghost-girl's voice.

"Yes." Davia managed another breath. "I...I don't want to...think about it."

"You have felt shame, too, then?"

Davia looked away. "My mother...she almost died...I didn't call." Coughing, coughing still. "I was a coward." She shook her head, blinked back tears. "Like you."

Emilie backed away. If the scent of gardenias still hung in the room, Davia could not smell it. Even so, her coughing eased off. After a minute or two, she could breathe freely again. "Thank you," she said.

"I did nothing."

Davia felt unmasked before Emilie. "I-I'm sorry. I'm as bad as you are."

"Perhaps not so bad. Perhaps only...human?"

Davia nodded, biting back a grin. "That's funny, coming from a ghost."

"Your mother, she has recovered?"

"For now." She breathed again, let the rest of the memory come. "How did I know she was bleeding inside? Even the ambulance guys, they didn't know. Six bags of blood she needed! If only I'd called..."

"You would have saved mere minutes, Davia. She must have been bleeding for days."

"Over a week, they said. From an ulcer she got after surgery."

"Then it was not your fault. Surely your parents do not blame you."

"They say they don't, but they're just being nice," Davia said. "I know I disappointed them."

"You were only a child. If they cannot see this, then they are fools. Surely you understand that you must forgive yourself." Emilie's words sounded vaguely familiar. But Davia couldn't remember who might have said them to her. Maybe it was Miss Teri.

"I wish I could," she said.

Emilie nodded. "I know this feeling. That is what I pray for—forgiveness. May God will it, someday I will rest in peace."

"Maybe you should take your own advice," Davia said. "Maybe *you* need to forgive yourself, too." She shrugged.

Emilie did not answer.

"Someone once told me that forgiveness is really a gift you give to yourself. It frees you from the pain of a past you cannot change. Or something like that." Yes, it *was* Miss Teri. Davia tried to remember if her therapist had said more. "Oh, yeah. And you can forgive without forgetting. It's really your choice."

"I will never forgive my parents, Davia," Emilie said fiercely. "It is their fault, what I did."

"But they didn't make you kill yourself," Davia pointed out. "You did. I bet they thought they were doing what was right."

"Well, they were wrong."

"Maybe my parents were, too—leaving me alone with Mom. But I think they were doing the best they could, Emilie. Yours, too."

"I do know they loved me," Emilie murmured.

"Maybe you've got to forgive *every*body who hurt you in the past. Including you."

Emilie looked thoughtful. "I cannot change what I did, that is for certain."

"Neither can I," Davia said.

Emilie crossed to the baby's crib and appeared to gently pat the swaddled infant's back. Davia continued to ponder what Miss Teri had told her about forgiveness. By the time Emilie returned to Davia, all Miss Teri's words made sense.

"*We* do the forgiving, Emilie," Davia said. "We can choose to. It's up to us and nobody else." *The Wizard of Oz* was playing out all over again, she realized. Dorothy had gone to see the Wizard and waited around for *his* help. But, like Davia and Emilie, she had possessed the ruby slippers all the time.

Davia felt like dancing. She held out her arms and spun around. "Come on, Emilie. Twirl with me!"

Emilie resisted for a moment, but finally she, too, flung her arms open. Side by side, they whirled around and around. Emilie's long dark hair splayed out behind her. Davia felt hers do the same. Their laughter bounced around the room. Dizzy at last, they collapsed on the floor.

Finally, they stood. Davia opened her arms to hug Emilie. When they embraced, she realized with a start that she was really hugging herself.

In the moment after Emilie stepped back, her expression changed, went soft, and melted into the widest smile Davia had ever seen. *"Merci*, Davia," she said. *"Au revoir."*

The glowing white of Emilie's dress hurt Davia's eyes now, but she couldn't look away. She reached out to the ghost-girl as Emilie had once reached out for her. And as she did, the house seemed to exhale. Davia's eyelids squeezed shut; her skin stretched tight. Then, stillness. And calm. She felt like Dorothy must have, in the middle of the cyclone. When she opened her eyes and looked around again, the house was dark, and the air reeked of smoke from zillions of candles that had burned brightly only moments before.

Emilie was gone.

CHAPTER 15

"Emilie?" Even as Davia called her name, she knew there'd be no answer. Silence roared in her ears. The Big House curled around her like a gigantic conch shell. Inside its fresh darkness, she felt suddenly lost and alone.

She groped along the wall. The air seemed heavier and warmer than she remembered. A musty smell sifted through the house. As she peered into the darkness, something tickled her nose. She sneezed three times, fast.

She thought of Aunt Mari lying so still on the bed, and felt a catch in her throat. I'm coming, Aunt Mari. Wait for me!

She sensed her way through the darkness to the stairs. Then, one hand firmly on the banister, she hurried down. Slivers of pink morning sliced through the downstairs curtains and guided Davia back to the parlor. She let herself look one last time—quickly—at the words Emilie had scratched on the window. They were still there, but in the first light of day, she noticed something else. Dust had already gathered on the piano and music rack. And cobwebs hung like long feather boas in the doorway.

Hurry!

With all her strength, Davia strong-armed the huge front doors. As she heaved the chains up from the porch, relocked them, and sucked the damp morning air deep into her lungs, everything inside her seemed to grow lighter.

Gratefully, she inhaled the new day.

***

"Thank goodness!" Dad said, when Davia came charging into the stable. He and Mom were still seated beside Aunt Mari's bed, exactly where Davia had left them. "Where in the world did you go? For a walk? At this hour?"

"Sort of." She was panting though, and sweaty. "Sorry for not leaving a note."

"It's not like you to go off like that, honey," Mom said. "We were so worried."

"I had to go to the Big House and do something for Aunt Mari. See?" She held up the keys. "I wasn't gone long."

"Come here." Mom held her arms out to Davia, bundled her in. Davia breathed in her sweet vanilla smell. "Are you okay?"

"Mmm-hmm," Davia whispered into Mom's neck. Finally, she eased away and turned toward the bed, to Aunt Mari. To her relief, she saw the covers move, but only slightly. GG, snuggled up against the old woman, didn't even raise her head.

"We haven't left her side for a minute," Dad said.

"Maybe she's waiting for you to leave," Davia said. "Isn't that what Paula said happens some-times?"

Mom nodded. "Or maybe she was waiting for you to come."

Davia let that thought sink in. She hoped it was true. "You guys go on," she said. "I'll sit with her for a while."

"Are you sure, sweetie?" Mom's eyes teared sud-denly and she looked away. At last, she touched Davia's cheek. Her fingers felt like rose petals. Then, turning to Dad, she said, "Ken, let's go." She moved her chair back and stood. "You call us if you need us," she whispered to Davia. Then she leaned over Aunt Mari, close to her ear. "Aunt Mari, Ken and I are going to take a little break. It's okay to let go, if you're ready, and you want to, when we're not here. We"—Mom's voice caught—"We love you and...and—"

"We're going to miss you, Aunt Mari," Dad added huskily. "Davia's here. You're not alone."

Davia sat down in Mom's chair. She still felt her

mother's warmth as she reached for Aunt Mari's hand. "Aunt Mari, it's me." She leaned in closer, whispering in the old woman's ear. "I just came from the Big House. Emilie's gone. Forever."

Just then, Aunt Mari squeezed her hand. Or maybe it was only a muscle twitch. Davia couldn't be sure.

"We both forgave everybody."

Aunt Mari gave no indication that she had heard.

"Anyway, now Emilie can rest in peace. And so can you."

Aunt Mari didn't move, didn't open her eyes. Neither did GG.

"I-I'm going to put your keys back now," Davia said. "I locked up. Everything's fine. Exactly as it should be."

Crossing to the dresser, she let the keys clunk to the bottom of the brass box. Then she touched the urn that held Robert's ashes. Her fingers lingered there for a long moment, before she took her seat again and tried to warm Aunt Mari's cold, cold hand against her own cheek. Finally, she kissed the old woman's palm.

"Open your eyes, Aunt Mari," she whispered fiercely. "Open your eyes."

Aunt Mari's eyelids twitched, as if she were really trying to open them.

"I know you can hear me. Squeeze my hand again, okay?" Once more, Davia took Aunt Mari's hand in hers. "Please. I know you can do it."

Aunt Mari's fingers moved faintly against Davia's palm.

Davia pressed her lips together, tears welling. "I just want to tell you, I-I'm really glad I got to know you, Aunt Mari," she said.

Aunt Mari's Vaseline-slicked lips edged upward in the faintest of smiles.

"Thank you," Davia whispered. "I promise I'll never forget you."

The old woman's breathing grew slower and slower, like an old clock someone had forgotten to wind. Davia held her breath when Aunt Mari did, and finally let hers go. When she looked again at Aunt Mari's face, she saw that her mouth had gone slack. And her covers weren't moving. Yellow sunlight sneaked under the shade and shone on her hair.

Davia gently let go of the old woman's hand. She stared at her aunt, lying motionless in the bed. She'd never seen a person be so still. But it wasn't Aunt Mari anymore, she realized. Not really. It was just her body. Her spirit was gone. Free.

Davia had expected she'd start shaking, or shrink away, or run crying for Mom and Dad. Instead, she sat and soaked up the silence. The peace.

Aunt Mari, where are you now?

Was she with Robert? Was she looking down on Davia? Was she like that ship sailing away? Davia closed her eyes, trying to feel her aunt's presence.

Little bells tinkled and, without warning, a firm weight landed in her lap.

GG!

The cat nuzzled in close, her head against Davia's heart, the one place she knew for sure Aunt Mari was right now. Could GG feel it beating and breaking at the same time?

"Oh, Aunt Mari," she whispered into GG's twitching ear, "I'm going to miss you."

GG walked her front paws up Davia's chest until her wet nose touched Davia's. A quick, rough tongue brushed her cheek. A kiss, at last, from her stubborn little 'fraidy cat! Hot tears burned Davia's eyes. She blinked at GG, and those amazing blue eyes blinked right back.

Flame-blue eyes, Davia noticed now. Like Aunt Mari's. Steady, direct, unwavering.

"Mom, Dad," she called at last, cradling GG in her arms like a baby. "Aunt Mari's..." Davia couldn't bring herself to say *dead*. She felt certain the real Aunt Mari was living on. "It's time to call hospice."

Her parents rushed in.

"Are you okay?" Dad asked, and Davia nodded.

Mom slipped her arm around Davia's waist and

squeezed her close. Pausing beside Aunt Mari's bed, Dad bowed his head for several moments, and then went to the kitchen to make the call.

When he returned, Mom took Davia's right hand and Dad took her left. Together they approached Aunt Mari's bed—Mom and Davia on one side, Dad on the other. Reaching across, their arms formed an unbroken circle that framed the old woman's face.

Davia felt GG rubbing against her legs.

Tears glazed Mom's cheeks. They reminded Davia of Emilie's. Looking up, Mom whispered, "Thank you for this life."

Davia wasn't sure whose life Mom was talking about—Aunt Mari's, Davia's, or her own. Maybe all of their lives. Or maybe just Life, in general.

"Thank you from me, too," Davia added. She felt certain that someone was listening.

Maybe even Aunt Mari.

CHAPTER 16

Mom and Dad were still in their bedroom, packing. But Davia had been ready to leave *Belle Forêt* for hours. She'd even gotten up early enough to watch the sun rise, pink and gold, in the east, where she knew New Orleans was trying hard to live again. Now she sat on the hide-a-bed, rereading the summer journal she was supposed to turn in to her eighth-grade core teacher in September. To be honest, she hadn't written that much in it, except for the list of things that scared her.

She could probably cross a lot of them off now.

Davia grinned down at GG. She was curled up in her crate, head on her paws, and they hadn't even given her a pill. Amazing.

Impatient, she called to her parents again, "Aren't you guys ready yet?"

"We will be by the time you find GG and put her in her crate," Dad called back.

"Ha. She's already in it," Davia said. "And she came all by herself."

Mom appeared in the hallway, wheeling her suitcase. "My, my. Miracles never cease."

Putting her journal away, Davia surveyed the great room to make sure she hadn't forgotten anything.

Oh, no! Aunt Mari's notebooks! Tenderly, she took them from the bookshelf and placed them in a special zippered pocket of her suitcase. She was going to do everything she could to put those pages in order again. Someday she'd pass them on to her own kid.

Mom took one last look in the fridge to make sure it was empty. Then she pulled out the electric plug and propped the door ajar with a dish towel.

Dad rolled the other suitcases into the front hall. "No regrets, Katie," he asked, "about letting this place go?"

Mom shook her head. "This isn't home," she said. "Not really. Madison is."

Davia remembered how at first she'd wanted to escape from *Belle Forêt*. But later, when Aunt Mari had told her all those stories about the LeBlancs, how romantic it had all sounded! Even during her encounters with Emilie, Davia had felt as if she were in her own little cocoon here. Not in real life at all. But now she couldn't wait to load the car and get on the road.

It seemed incredible that they'd be back in Madison in time for the annual Fourth of July "Rhythm and Booms" fireworks. And a couple of days after that, she'd be leaving for French camp. They'd had a cancellation, so she could go there for the rest of the summer.

"Okay," Dad said, "are we ready to roll?"

Davia glanced back toward Aunt Mari's room. She saw the brass box, her aunt's antique perfume bottles, and the silver mirror and brush still on the dresser. Mom had managed to pack up all Aunt Mari's clothes in the busy days after the funeral. She'd decided to donate them and a lot of other stuff to hospice's resale shop. But she had never touched the things on Aunt Mari's dresser—except Robert's ashes, of course, which were scattered with Aunt Mari's under the oaks, exactly as she'd wanted.

"Mom, come here for a minute, will you?" She motioned her mother into Aunt Mari's room. The cut-crystal bottles glittered in the new morning sun. How she'd love to be able to hold Aunt Mari's brush—to put her hands where Aunt Mari had— and to look into the same mirror as her aunt had all her life. And even though the brass box no longer held the keys to the Big House, it seemed to contain Davia's memories of a summer that had probably changed her life. "Would it be okay if we take these home with us?"

"Of course," Mom said, and tweaked Davia's chin. "I think Aunt Mari would like that a lot."

Carefully, she and Mom packed up Aunt Mari's last treasures.

"Come out, come out, wherever you are!" Dad called. "Are you ladies ready?"

Davia could see her father framed in the front doorway—a silhouette, almost, against a square of sunny sky. She glanced around the room one last time—and finally out the window at the *garçon-nière*. Then, hugging the bundle against her heart, she slipped her free hand in Mom's.

"Ready or not," she called back, "here we come!"

"Things I, Davia Ann Peters, Am Afraid Of"

1. ~~death~~
2. ~~ghosts~~
3. ~~strange places~~
4. ~~strangers~~
5. ~~being alone~~
6. Mom's cancer coming back
7. ~~fire~~
8. snakes
9. losing friends
10. ~~making new ones~~
11. hurricanes
12. alligators
13. tornados
14. ~~cemeteries~~
15. giving oral reports
16. ~~getting laughed at~~
17. ~~a bad asthma attack~~
18. ~~what I'd have to do to be a doctor, though I~~
~~think I'd really like to be one~~
19. ~~the dark~~
20. ~~being responsible for someone else~~
21. ~~my cat never liking me~~

SHERI SINYKIN

is the author of several books for young readers, including the upcoming picture book Z<small>AYDE</small> C<small>OMES</small> <small>TO</small> L<small>IVE</small>. She holds degrees from Stanford University and Vermont College, where she received an MFA in writing for children. She lives in Wisconsin and Arizona. Please visit her website at *www.sherisinykin.com.*